SAMANTHA HONEYCOMB

"Enchanting and full of joy."
Inner Self

Other Titles by *Scott Zarcinas*

Your Natural State of Being

SCOTT ZARCINAS

SAMANTHA HONEYCOMB

A Pilgrim's Chronicle

ꝛ
DoctorZed Publishing

DoctorZed Publishing
86 Valley View Drive, Highbury
South Australia 5089

DoctorZed Publishing website address is:
www.doctorzed.com

This DoctorZed International edition published 2008

A CIP record for this book can be found at the
National Library of Australia

Parent ISBN: 192120702-7
International ISBN: 0 9775969 3 1

Printed and bound in UK and USA by
lightningsource.co.uk

Cover Photograph by Creacart
www.istockphoto.com
file no. 935057

For My Girls

ACKNOWLEDGMENTS

This book could not have come into existence without the loving support of Dr. Martie Botha. Her patience and faith go far beyond the call of duty. Beyond her marriage vows, in any case. I know of few women who are prepared to suffer the stings and arrows of outrageous dreams. Few husbands have had it so lucky.

I extend my gratitude to Megan Davidson for her early editorial of the manuscript. Her critique made this book more technically correct than a mere writer could have ever hoped to achieve. The reader has her to thank for Mad Jack's survival.

I would also like to thank the many individuals who were kind enough to review the manuscript and provide an input to its metamorphosis.

Lastly, to God, who is always helping me to be my best, whether I like it or not.

"Something is nothing and nothing is something."

GERALD THE GREAT

PART ONE

SAMANTHA B. HONEYCOMB buzzed around the garden admiring the hundreds of rose buds spread out before her. Only one thing occupied her mind of late: flowers. Tulips, roses, geraniums, lilies, orchids, pink ones, blue ones, red ones, yellow ones – she loved them all – but every day, it seemed, she changed her mind as to which one she favored. One day it was yellow pansies, the next day orange tulips, today red roses. There were just *so* many.

How terrible, she thought, hovering over the rose bed, that a teenage honeybee couldn't decide which flower she liked most.

She buzzed toward a rose the color of crimson fire. It seemed to welcome her closer, wanting to embrace her with its petals, and when she inhaled its perfume she was lifted away in a glorious, dreamy haze.

"I wouldn't even think about it if I were you," said a worker bee buzzing past. "You know the rules."

Though taken off guard, Samantha smiled and nodded politely, watching the worker bee buzz out of sight to some other part of the garden. She knew the rules all right. What bee didn't? Everyone not of the Sisterhood was strictly forbidden to enter the heart of a rose, the *corolla*, and there was nothing she could do about it. It had been that way for ever and ever, and it was a constant source of conflict with her mother. They'd even had an argument as recently as this morning over breakfast, in the kitchen of the hive-cell.

"Why is it a sacrilege to gather nectar from a rose?" she had asked.

Isabeella was readying herself for a hard day's toil, making sure her wings were in working order, flapping them in short bursts every so often, wiping dust from her stripes, checking that her pollen sacks were clean and free of holes; doing everything, it seemed, to evade the question.

Samantha was well used to her mother's delaying tactics, and she wasn't going to give up that easily. She asked again, and Isabeella smiled, as if in resignation. A trying smile, Samantha thought, knowing what she was going to say next, what she always said in such circumstances: "Because, Samantha, just because."

Samantha stared at her, not content to let it be. She wished her father was there to help her out, but he was still in bed. That was another thing she didn't understand: only females gathered nectar. The drones just made sure the hive was kept nice and tidy and sometimes moonlighted as guards or cleaners to earn some extra honey. A lucky few, when summoned to the palace, kept the queen amused with tales of victorious battles and ballads of forbidden, sensual love. Reginald Honeycomb was particularly famous for his rendition of the epic battle of the War of the Wasps, a story the queen never tired of hearing. "He's never had a *real* job", her mother had often complained (he had been chosen to stay in the queen's harem as a younger drone, until he was too old to perform his duties; then he found a wife and slept late every morning). Samantha had to agree – he certainly lived the good life – yet it bugged her that bees who entertained for a living had it much easier than those who had to labor in the garden for their honey. When she was older, she promised herself, she was going to be a performer, or a queen, or whatever came first.

At that moment, though, she had greater things on her mind. "Why are roses sacred?" she asked again.

Isabeella plonked the nectar sack on the table, scowling. "Because they belong to the Sisterhood."

"Even the wild roses that grow near the border with the Crazy Lands?" Samantha asked.

Isabeella sighed. "Even those."

It wasn't fair, Samantha thought. There was no good reason why the Sisterhood should own every rose in the queendom while lay bees couldn't have any. The law was stupid and it was wrong. She was going to do something about it.

"Why do you want to gather rose nectar, anyway?" Isabeella asked. "It's no different than tulip or orchid or geranium nectar, and you can gather as much of that as you like." Her tone, if Samantha didn't know better, bordered on patronizing. "Besides, the rules are the rules," her mother added. "There's a reason the laws are written the way they are, and it's not for worker bees like us to ask why. There's no point in trying to change them. Not even the queen would do that."

"You're wrong!" Samantha said, and clenched her claws until they hurt. "I'm going to go to the queen and I'm going to ask her to change the law so that every bee can own a rose, too."

"Next thing you know, you'll want to change the law so that drones can work with females. How ridiculous," her mother said. "The law is the law and you'd do well to know your place and accept it." With that said, she left for work.

How often she had wished things were different, Samantha thought now, staring into the rose. It was the law and there was nothing she could do to change that. But, oh, how she yearned to enter its corolla. Was she never going to know what it was like? She wondered why the Great Mother Bee, the Creator of the entire universe, would give the world roses if only the Sisterhood were allowed to enjoy them. Wasn't it true that bees were around for millions and millions of years before flowers even existed? If so, wouldn't that mean that they were a gift for *every* bee?

Then a tempting thought made her giggle. What if she entered while no one was looking? It was an outrageous idea. Did she have the courage to do it? She looked around, left and right, over her wings, behind her stinger, and saw no sign of anyone else. Except, in the distance, in the direction of the hills and the setting sun, she saw a kite gliding on the wind. The pilot was obscured behind the maple tree on which the hive was hanging, most probably one of the humans that lived in the farmhouse nearby. The kite soared in the air, far, far higher than she'd ever dared to go herself, almost to the very clouds, a swirling red petal lifted higher and higher on invisible wings.

One day, she wished, she would buzz as high as the clouds too, maybe even higher.

She turned back to the rose below. If she was going to enter its corolla, it was now or never. The fear of being caught, however, was like a wing-shackle. Her wings were suddenly heavy and an effort to flap. If she were caught inside the rose, she would be summoned before the queen, that was for certain. Then what? Punishment of some kind, most probably. Imprisonment, execution, she didn't know exactly. No one had broken the ancient law, ever, as far as she knew. No one had dared. Perhaps it was better if she didn't.

She was about to turn and buzz away when she heard a voice. It seemed to be coming from the crimson rose, as if the Great Mother Herself was speaking directly to her. "Samantha," the voice said, ever so faintly. "Be a bee. Sip the Nectar of Life."

The temptation was just too much. Samantha Honeycomb landed on its welcoming petal and entered its secret and forbidden realm.

THE MOMENT SAMANTHA emerged from the rose, three worker bees buzzed overhead. Her eyes widened in alarm. From the looks on their faces she knew she was in trouble, even more than when she enrolled in aerobatic flying school instead of attending hive-economics (her mother had immediately removed her from the flying school when she eventually found out, and had made her clean the hive-cell as punishment, but by then Samantha had already learnt some quite spectacular stunts), and within the time it took to pull herself from the rose, several royal guards had already descended upon her. It was a bee's worst nightmare. The guards swarmed down from the sky like wasps attacking the hive. She didn't have time to hide. She didn't even have time to try a mosquito roll, a forward somersault with a double-twist and pike, or a blowfly back flip, a full reverse-loop with a half-twist, or any of the escape maneuvers she had learnt at flying school. The guards completely encircled her, thrusting their stingers only bee-inches from her chest and back and sides.

7

"We're arresting you on suspicion of poaching sacred nectar," said the captain of the guards, and Samantha's eyes widened further. "You're coming with us to Hive Prison young lady."

Two of them seized her wings, lifted her into the air, then began to haul her toward the maple tree and the hive.

It happened so quickly that she was halfway across the garden, past the spurting water fountain and pond in which the goldfish swam, past the bird-bath and the sandpit where the swallows and the blackbirds frolicked, past the outdoor table that the humans often used on summer afternoons, and past the patch of rosemary, coriander, sage, and basil, before she even had time to wiggle her antennae. She barely registered the shock of the workers that had stopped gathering nectar to watch what was happening.

Almost at the maple tree, she heard her name being called. Her mother was hovering over a large geranium bush, staring in disbelief. A sack of nectar slipped from her grasp, bouncing off several petals before splattering onto the grass beneath.

"Where are they taking you?" Isabeella asked. "What have you done?"

Only now did Samantha realize the trouble she was in. She wanted to reply, but her voice seemed to have been captured too. She wanted to say that she was sorry she didn't listen to her advice this morning. She wanted to say that she was scared, that she didn't want to be taken to the dungeons, but her voice remained stuck and the guards didn't slow. Then she was at the maple tree, and her mother's calls were lost in the rustle of wind through its leaves.

Samantha glanced up, almost too frightened to look. Hanging from a high branch was the hive of the eastern queendom. It had never looked so daunting. The entrance yawned like some unspeakable monster from the Crazy Lands; and as she passed through, several sentries glared at her with suspicion. She felt very small, like a young grub being reared in the nursery. Her wings flapped nervously and her legs trembled, but it only got worse inside. The lower level was buzzing with activity, by far the busiest of the hive's seven levels. Bees entering and exiting the gates stopped to stare, much to her dismay, and though the chamber was illuminated via small air vents in the honeycombed walls, it felt uncommonly dark and cool. Samantha shivered and trembled even more, thinking, for some reason, that her wings were feeling particularly brittle and fragile.

The guards set her down and marched her deeper into the hive. Samantha struggled forward, still unable to comprehend what was happening. Just above and ahead of her was the central beeway, the chimney-like corridor that divided each level into two sectors, east and west, and on any normal day Samantha would ascend it to her hive-cell on the third level on the inner western side, the working-class neighborhood just across from the large pollen and nectar storage sites of the honey factories. Except this day had suddenly become anything but normal. It had mutated into something distinctly abnormal, with a capital A.

Some bees descending from an upper level stopped and stared before heading to the market over in the eastern sector. Samantha recalled the countless hours spent wandering through the sprawling maze of the Grand Beezaar, where anything and everything was for sale; beautiful caterpillar silks from the southern queendom; exotic pollens and nectars from the west; woodcraft — hiveware and furniture and such like — from the carpenter bees that lived somewhere near the Crazy Lands; gardening equipment from the bumblebees; and, of course, the one thing every bee desired (and the ants and wasps and aphids and termites, and just about every other insect Samantha knew about), honey: the common bond that united every creature in the known world, the very reason the Grand Beezaar was the busiest place in the whole hive. Samantha usually loved the aromas of pollens and nectars and beeswax and honey, the tireless buzz and energy, but today it felt somewhat menacing, like a mob on the verge of rioting.

Samantha suddenly felt the sharp point of a stinger between her wings. She stumbled forward, almost falling over. "Stop staring and get moving," the captain said, prodding her again. "You know where the dungeons are."

Like every honeybee in the hive, her wing-spines prickled at the mention of the dungeons. She had heard many rumors of what happened inside: torture, starvation, disease, and any number of horrors. Bees entered that unspeakable place and were never heard of again.

With legs still trembling, Samantha was marched to the front of Hive Prison. The walls loomed over her, almost touching the ceiling of the lower level. The gates were just as high; and hanging from them was a cage, inside of which was a rotting exoskeleton, yawning (or was it screaming?) back at her, its claws still gripping the bars. Samantha stood immobilized with terror. Even her hearing seemed to have seized, for as if from the other side of the hive she heard the captain yelling for the gate to be opened. Several seconds later, it creaked ajar.

"Move!" the captain said, prodding her again.

A waft of stench drifted past. Samantha didn't budge, her petrified legs stuck to the ground as if she were standing deep in a vat of honey.

Then, after a brief moment, she felt herself being picked up from under her wings and hauled into the prison.

IT WAS PITCH black behind the gate.

When her eyes adjusted, she saw that she was being taken across a narrow bridge that spanned a deep, dark pit smelling of rotting carcasses. Another door was opened on the other side of the bridge, smaller and more conventional than the main prison gates. The guards took Samantha through it into a dank tunnel that dripped a treacle-like substance from its ceiling, a substance Samantha hoped wasn't the liquefied remnants of some prisoner's entrails.

They emerged into a large courtyard surrounded by four low tiers of prison cells, as many as five to six hundred in total. She was dragged to the other side of the courtyard and thrown onto the cold, hard floor of a cell. It smelled of vomit and bee-dung, and for a moment she lay there, stunned. She heard the prison guard laugh and the slamming of the door, followed quickly by the jingle of keys and the clunk of the lock.

After a short while, Samantha picked herself up and slumped her tired body onto the bed beneath the window. She had little or no energy, too tired even for tears, so she just lay there, even though the straw mattress stabbed her wings and legs and made it impossible to get comfortable. Time passed extraordinarily slowly. For what seemed hours, she wondered what she was going to do. Her thoughts also drifted to her godmother, the bee she'd always turned to for advice when she was feeling lonely or down.

"The Great Mother would want you to learn from this," she imagined the wise old bee saying. "She has a plan for every bee in the world and She makes sure that everything happens for a reason."

Samantha questioned whether she could really believe in a Grand Plan. It seemed that that sort of thing only happened in fairytales, to heroines falling in love with handsome princes, never in real life to an everyday bee like herself. Why would the Great Mother bother with someone like her, anyway? She wasn't important. She was never going to change the world. Samantha drew a deep breath and sighed. It was too difficult to see the meaning in everything that happened, and much easier to believe that she was simply the victim of circumstance.

Then she remembered another piece of advice from her godmother. "When I was searching for meaning, I was like a bee on a tulip petal looking for a tulip." She had then paused and smiled. "So my advice to you, young lady, is this: When you are searching for meaning, look no further than where you are."

Samantha had to admit she didn't really understand what her godmother had meant, but she supposed there was no harm in trying to follow her advice, and so began to cast an eye over her new living quarters. There was not much there – a straw bed, a bucket, and a stool – and above her head on the adjacent wall, a bright white- and black- striped square cast by a ray of dusty light filtering through the bars of the cell's solitary window. *No, not much here at all, really*, she thought.

The cell's grim reality made her feel even more depressed; and as she contemplated her miserable lot, something caught her eye, a shadow on the wall, like a black fly buzzing back and forth. At first she didn't know what to make of it, and then she realized that something was flying past the window. She sprung onto the bed and peered through the bars.

The window, surprisingly, looked directly outside the hive. Through the branches and leaves of the maple tree, she was able to see what was casting the shadow, a red, diamond-shaped kite, swaying to and fro in the sky. Who or what, she couldn't make out, was piloting it in the field of tall grass that spread west toward the hills of the Crazy Lands. When the kite passed back again, its shadow cross- ed her face. Watching it soar filled her with a quiet sense of joy. She momentarily forgot her prison cell, flying free with the kite.

Then quite unexpectedly, it stalled in flight. With- in the beat of a wing, it plunged toward the ground, spiraling and spiraling and spiraling until it dived into the tall grass and was lost to sight.

Samantha waited for it to rise again. After ten or so minutes she gave up and lay back down on the bed, then curled into a tight ball and cried herself to sleep.

THE TRIAL DATE was set for one week.

Samantha was allowed no visitors, not even her parents, and she had to make do with only one meal a day, stale honeybread and water. The wait was unbearable. Often she whiled away the hours peering through the bars in the hope of spotting the kite again, but she never did. It only got worse. As the trial date neared, she became even more agitated and anxious. She couldn't sit still for a moment, as almost every minute was spent dreading what was to become of her. If she had to spend the rest of her life in this prison cell, she thought she would go as mad as a wasp. Execution would be more merciful.

As it was, she was already having strange and unusual dreams, and on the night before the trial she had the oddest one of all. Seated in the middle of an old theatre, Samantha found herself surrounded by rows and rows of empty seats. Ahead, on the bare stage, an old actress sat on a single chair. Apart from Samantha, the actress, who looked remarkably similar to her godmother, was the only bee in the whole place.

"Hello Samantha," the actress said, "what scene would you like me to act?"

Samantha didn't know many plays, but she was aware of a famous writer who'd apparently written some pretty good stuff. "What about some William Shakesbee?" she said, hoping this to be sufficient.

"My, my," the actress said, and paused, trying to remember her lines. "All right, let me see what I can do for you." She went to the edge of the stage, then puffed her chest, tilted her head, and said: "There are more mysteries, Horatio Bee, in hive-heaven than can be dreamt in your hive."

The actress stood frozen, waiting for applause, but it was a number of seconds before Samantha realized what she was meant to do. "Bravo! Bravo!" she said, clapping. "Bravo!"

The actress looked very pleased and dropped a curtsy. She turned to face the absent audience and gestured for silence. "To bee or not to bee, that is the question." She flapped her wings to stress the point. "Is it better to suffer the stings and arrows of outrageous fortune, or oppose them?"

"Bravo! Bravo!" Samantha applauded again, this time with more vim. "Encore! Encore!"

The actress shook her head. "You now know all you need to know," she said. "There is no more I can teach you. It is now up to you to go and bee."

Samantha woke early the next morning with one thought buzzing through her mind: *To bee or not to bee.* She was still lying on her bed, wondering what in the world it could mean, when she heard movement outside her door, then the rattle of keys, and then the unlocking of the door. The prison guard walked in, followed by the captain of the royal guards. "Get up!" the captain said. "It's time."

Samantha sat up straight away. She suddenly felt very awkward. She looked shabby and smelled rather grim, really in no state to go to trial, but the captain was having none of it. She was hauled outside the cell, where five more guards were waiting to escort her to the courtrooms. Two in front, two behind, and one on each side, she was marched out of Hive Prison to the central bee-way and the long walk to the fifth level.

It seemed that word had spread that a poacher had been caught with her claws in sacred nectar, for many bees had taken position along the route to witness the procession, a once in a lifetime event.

The size of the crowd was somewhat daunting. Six guards felt rather inadequate for her protection, and although most of the crowd watched her pass in silence, she heard some nasty comments from several older drones in front of the nursery on the second level, reinforcing her fears.

"Rot in jail!" shouted one, shaking his clenched claw at her.

"Prison's too good for you!" said another.

Their comments were followed with murmurs of approval.

Samantha's fear grew the closer she got to the courtroom, as did the numbers in the crowd. On the third level, onlookers were lining the bee-way almost three deep. The air was thick with the smells of pollen and nectar from the factories, smells that were as familiar as home-baked honeybread but unfortunately only reminded her of the hardships she was suffering. She was struck with a pang of homesickness, and desperately scanned the crowd for her mother and father. Unable to see them, she wondered where they were. It would be a terrible humiliation for them. Would they attend the trial or stay inside their hive-cell? She could hardly expect them to show their faces in public, yet she knew she couldn't go through this alone. She'd never wanted so much to be with them in all her short life.

The guards then led her through the central bees-nest district on the fourth level. The crowd was now five or six deep. Samantha even caught many faces looking down on her from the old nests, the tallest of which touched the ceiling nine or ten cells high. Hundreds, if not thousands, of pairs of eyes were staring at her. A newspaper drone was selling this morning's paper, hot off the press.

"Get your Daily Bee!" he shouted above the restless crowd. "Trial of the Century starts today! Read all about it!" It seemed he couldn't sell them fast enough.

Samantha finally arrived at the courthouse in the eastern sector of the fifth level, where a menacing crowd had gathered with placards demanding her immediate execution. As the guards led her on by, Samantha heard someone shout, "There she is!" The crowd surged forward, baying and screaming and shouting obscenities. Samantha thought she was going to be ripped apart, but the guards closed ranks and pushed a path through the unruly mob. A moment later, she felt one of her wings being grabbed. Her squeals alerted the guards, who shoved the offending bee to the ground, and then marched on.

It was a struggle, but after a few minutes they were inside the courthouse. The doors were barred and they hastened down the empty corridor to Courtroom 3. Samantha breathed a sigh of relief, but her reprieve was only momentary. To her dismay, the tiny chamber was packed with hundreds of bees. Reporters had taken over the whole section behind the witness stand, some already writing on their pads, and the upper and lower levels of the public gallery were crammed. The low hum that was reverberating around the room hushed when she entered. Her wings flapped and she buzzed fretfully, a childhood habit she'd never outgrown, and now wished she had.

Not wanting to look at the crowd, Samantha eyed the queen's golden throne. It sat empty on a high dais backing the far wall, on which a portrait of the queen herself was hanging, Queen Beetrix Bee IV. From the seat beneath the dais, the magistrate watched her every step as the guards led her to the prisoner's stand directly opposite. The room was still hushed.

"Prisoner in the docks!" the captain shouted.

Samantha cringed with embarrassment. Turning, she glimpsed the frightened faces of her mother and father in the upper gallery behind her. She was glad they were here. Her mother tried to smile, but her face was wracked with worry. A murmur then began buzzing around the chamber.

"All rise!" said the magistrate, and the room echoed with the thuds and scrapes of hundreds of bees standing as one.

After a moment, the queen duly entered from a door behind the dais and sat on her throne. Queen Beetrix Bee IV was judge, jury and executioner, and Samantha could see she wasn't in a happy mood. The rest of the courtroom then sat down, except Samantha; there was no seat for the prisoner in the docks, so she remained standing, head bowed. This was the moment she'd been dreading.

Soon, she'd know whether she was to live or die.

"SAMANTHA B. HONEYCOMB," bellowed the magistrate. "You stand charged before Her Majesty, Queen Beetrix Bee the Fourth, with unlawful trespass, poaching and wanton disregard for the law. Do you wish to respond or plea before the proceedings commence?"

An expectant hush lingered in the air. Samantha said nothing, just shook her head. The prosecution then called the first of the three bees who'd stumbled upon her as she emerged (allegedly) from the crimson rose, covered from head to stinger in pollen.

"I guess at first we didn't want to believe it," the witness said. To Samantha, she looked tired and worn out, a worker bee that had come to the end of her wearisome life. "I had already warned her not to trespass on sacred ground. I was shocked when I came back and saw her. She had no right to go in there."

The other witnesses were just as reproachful. One of them even dared to call upon the queen to sentence Samantha to death. It was greeted with an approving buzz from a certain section of the gallery, placard-waving members of the Committee for Beenevolence, otherwise known as the CB's. Worse, the prosecution then stood and called a surprise witness.

"I call the Guardian of Truth," the prosecuting lawyer said, a bee with hairy antennae and a bad habit of picking dirt from her claws with her stinger when she thought nobody was looking. "Her Most Eternally Venerate, the Holy Eminent Designate of the Sacred Order, the High Priestess Bee."

Samantha heard reverent gasps among the crowd. Even the queen seemed to be in awe of the Priestess as she entered and took the witness stand. Most bees had never seen her in the flesh, including Samantha. The Priestess rarely left the confines of the cathedral, and it was clear she was not amused to be called as a witness. Samantha caught her scornful look as she placed her claw on the Holy Beeble and swore to tell the truth, the whole truth, and nothing but the truth, so help her Mighty Goddess.

"Your Holy Eminence," the prosecuting lawyer said with reverence, "would you please tell the court why the laws strictly forbid worker bees to trespass on sacred ground?"

The High Priestess sighed. "Very well," she said. "As the Guardian of Truth, it is my solemn duty to safeguard the Secrets of Life. You could say that this is the fundamental concern of the Sisterhood."

"And why is that?"

"Is it not true that bees were around for millions of years before flowers even existed?" she asked. The crowd, including the magistrate and Queen Beetrix, murmured in affirmation. "Then flowers, especially roses, are extremely precious, are they not?" Again everyone murmured in agreement. "The Great Mother didn't just bestow Her gifts onto everybody, did she? No! She gave us her precious gifts so that we would take proper care of them. If the Secrets of Life were to fall into the wrong claws, *evil* claws," and here she turned and glared at Samantha, "chaos would take over the hive." Then her mouth parted in a smile that made Samantha think of an executioner's grin. "And if that were to happen," she said, "then death would surely befall all of us."

Samantha gulped as her gaze darted around the room. Everyone, including the queen, was nodding in agreement. A chorus of boos rose from the CB's who, up until that point, had been overwhelmed into silence.

"The heart of a rose is sacred because it holds the key to the Secret of Life," the Priestess said, her initial reluctance to take the stand now replaced by eager righteousness. "In its honey gland, what we of the Sisterhood know as its *nectary*, lies the sweet essence of the Goddess. It is found in no other flower. This essence is one of the key ingredients that the Sisterhood, with a secret and holy ritual, use to transform nectar into honey, the life-blood of the hive. Without this sacred essence we could have no honey, and without honey we would have no hive." She was in a frenzy of speech by now, her face seething with hatred. She slowly raised her hairy arm and pointed. "This bee has broken our ancient law and trespassed on holy ground. Will we allow her the opportunity to bring death and destruction upon us?"

"No!" shouted the gallery.

The High Priestess stood and faced the queen. "Then I beg your Majesty to ensure that she never gets the chance to do so." Without waiting to be dismissed, she stepped down from the witness box and left the courtroom, shouts of approval following her as she went.

Samantha knew her fate was sealed.

HOLDING BACK THE tears now welling in her eyes, Samantha's wings flapped and her legs trembled. It seemed to take an eternity for the courtroom to settle. "Do you have anything to say?" asked the magistrate.

Samantha didn't answer, too afraid to speak. Every possible outcome was a disaster. Why was this happening? Had she really done something so terrible? Suddenly, an old nursery rhyme she used to sing hummed in her mind:

> *I am a little honeybee*
> *And Samantha is my name.*
> *I buzz and sing and laugh at things*
> *'Coz to me its all the same.*

I like to fly as high as crows
Then dive into a rose,
'Coz a honeybee is not afraid
To bee what she is made.

"Do you have anything to say?" the magistrate asked again, shaking Samantha from her reverie.

When she said nothing, a restless hum buzzed throughout the chamber, gathering volume by the second.

"Enough!" the magistrate shouted. The audience hushed at once.

The queen was sitting patiently on her courtroom throne, contemplating Samantha's punishment. She gestured for the magistrate to be seated. "Before I pass sentence," she said to Samantha, "there's one thing I wish to know." Samantha looked up at the queen, terrified. "Why did you do it?"

To Samantha, the answer was as simple and as natural as buzzing through the gardens and fields. "I was called to do it," she said.

The whole audience sat with mouth agape. The reporter bees sitting behind the witness box, at first shocked, furiously wrote down every word and every detail.

"Who called you to break the law?" asked Queen Beetrix. "Name the bee who called you to do this terrible deed and I will spare you."

"Nobody made me break the law," Samantha said. "I did it on my own free will. It wasn't such a terrible thing, was it?"

The courtroom gasped and buzzed excitedly and the reporters were furiously scribing once again. SAMANTHA MOCKS THE LAW wrote one of them for tomorrow's headline. The CB's booed and demanded her immediate hanging.

"Silence in the courtroom!" the magistrate said, bellowing like a stung bull. "Silence at once!"

Queen Beetrix Bee IV waited until everyone was quiet before she spoke again. "Let me remind you that you have been found guilty of a crime that has no precedent in the history of the hive. This indeed makes it terrible." She paused, allowing Samantha to fully appreciate the seriousness of the situation. "I have no option than to have you detained in Hive Prison indefinitely, or for however long I deem to be worthy punishment. Do you understand?"

Samantha understood at once. Her life was over. Detained at Her Majesty's pleasure in the bowels of Hive Prison was a sentence worse than death. She would no longer smell the garden flowers, nor see them bloom in springtime. Everything she lived for was now to be taken away. She began to cry, and the courtroom looked on in disbelief. No one uttered a word.

"You will have plenty of time to contemplate the consequences of your actions," the queen said. "When I'm convinced that you have shown sufficient remorse for the crime you have committed, then I will consider an appeal for you to be allowed back into the colony."

Samantha sniffed and wiped away her tears, wondering what her godmother would say in such a moment of despair. Then the words just seemed to pop out of her mouth. "Everything happens for a reason," she said.

"What did you say?" Queen Beetrix said, leaning forward on her throne. "I can't hear you."

Samantha lifted her head and looked directly into her eyes. The renewed determination in her voice surprised even herself. "Everything happens for a reason," she said, this time loud enough for every bee in the courtroom to hear.

The reporters got busy once again and the queen's laugh was full of scorn. "Who taught you that, my dear girl? Everything happens because *I* say it will. That is the only reason. I have absolute power in this queendom – the power of life and death. Nothing happens without my consent."

"You're wrong!" Samantha said.

An audible groan lifted from the chamber, then someone from the CB's yelled for her tongue to be cut out. Her mother even shouted for her not to argue with the queen.

Samantha wasn't listening, not to her mother, not to the queen, only to her heart. Deep down she knew she didn't deserve this punishment. In fact, she was sure everyone including the queen knew she didn't deserve it, but no one was prepared to say what they believed was right. They all lived in fear of the High Priestess and were too afraid to make a stand for the truth.

Well, she was having none of it. If she was going to go to prison, then she wasn't going to go without a fight. She was going to let everybody know that what was happening today was wrong and could happen to any one of them tomorrow if they didn't do anything about it now. She recalled her dream from last night. This was her chance to bee or not to bee.

"There's a reason to everything," she said to the queen, "and it's determined by the Great Mother, not you."

The roar of disapproval almost shook the queen's portrait off its hook. Even the floor began to tremble. The reporters scribbled like mad and the magistrate bellowed for silence, without success. At some stage, Samantha heard a drone shout that someone had fainted (she discovered later that it was her mother). Then one of the CB's jumped over the railing with a placard held high above her head, bee-lining straight for the prisoner's docks. Before she got to Samantha, luckily, two guards blocked her path and escorted her out of the courtroom, kicking and yelling. It took several minutes before order was restored.

The queen took it all in her stride, seemingly amused. "Samantha, my dear child," she said, "you are young and naïve, and you are ignorant of the way this world works. This, I can forgive you for. I can not, however, forgive you for breaking the law."

"You do what you feel you must do," Samantha said, resigned to her fate, "but it will not change my belief. My life rests in the claws of Another."

The queen paused for a second, a curious glint in her black eyes. "Pray tell me," she said, "who is going to stop me from having you imprisoned, or executed, or even banished from the hive?" She didn't wait for an answer. "I will tell you, young lady: nobody. Your life lies in *my* royal claws, not yours, not anyone's, only mine."

Samantha nodded respectfully. "As your subject, I must accept your sentence," she said. "But I still believe that there is a higher reason than our own, including yours."

"We shall see, young lady, we shall see." The queen then nodded to the two guards standing on either side of the prisoner's docks. "Take her away!"

They escorted Samantha out of the courtroom with the howls and jeers of the gallery ringing in her ears. The mayhem was only brought under control when extra guard reinforcements arrived to escort the maddened throng outside. The reporter bees were to write that a riot had only just been averted.

But by then, Samantha was already locked away in Hive Prison.

SAMANTHA SAT IN the dark dungeon cell on the edge of the bed. Heavy with despair, her head drooped like a wilting sunflower and her wings flopped to her sides. She was faced with the undeniable truth that she was now a prisoner who had nothing; she had no hope of freedom, no chance of happiness, no foreseeable future to look forward to. If the Great Mother Bee had a reason for her suffering, she couldn't see it. It was frustrating, but she figured that if she didn't understand at this moment what it was she was supposed to learn, then perhaps she should just have the faith to believe that she *would* learn it at some other time, when she was *ready* to learn it.

Maybe, she mused, that was what was going on: her faith was being tested. Faith was kind of like knowledge in that sense. She could only show the teachers at bee-school how much she knew by writing exams. Likewise, she could only show the Great Mother how much faith she had by being tested, like now.

The idea slowly rekindled her hope that she would one day understand the reason for all her troubles. At that moment, she heard the rattle of keys outside. "You have work to do!" said the prison guard.

Before Samantha could reply, a worker bee with a large blue- and white-striped sack on her back entered and dumped it in the far corner. It didn't stop there. Bee after bee dumped similar sacks, one on top of the other in a pile that soon reached the ceiling. After the last bee had come and gone, the guard slammed the door and peered through its little barred window. "Finish them by this time next week, or you'll be punished!"

Samantha stared at the pile of sacks. Like a mound of large boulders, they took up almost a quarter of the whole cell. She untied one of them and peeked inside. It was filled with blue things with long legs and short arms. She removed one, unsure as to what to make of it. It was ripped and made of some kind of material she'd only ever seen humans wear. Inside was a tag: PRODUCT OF PROCRUSTE ANT INC. ONE SIZE FITS ALL.

"They're overalls," the guard said. "You'll find socks and antennae warmers in the other sacks, all ripped. Your job is to mend them. Now get to work!"

"What's Procruste Ant Incorporated?" Samantha asked. "Whose are all these clothes?"

The guard laughed and told her that that kind of information was strictly on a need to know basis. Samantha shrugged, spying a red toolbox next to the pile of sacks. Inside was a tray of needles, thimbles and scissors. She lifted out the tray and saw a delightful rainbow of color. Spools of thread littered the bottom of the box. Red, green, blue, yellow, orange – they reminded her of all the flowers in the queendom, especially the crimson rose that had lured her into its corolla. She glanced at the sacks, now wishing that she had attended hive-economics, like her mother had wanted, rather than aerobatic flying school. She was never going to be able to stitch up the whole lot within a week.

Nevertheless, what else could she do? If she didn't at least attempt it, she'd never finish. Sitting on her straw bed, she removed a needle, threaded it with blue yarn, and then set to work mending the overalls. By the time of the changing of the guards at midnight, Samantha had almost patched and sewed all the items in the sack.

She turned to the large blue- and white-striped mound in the corner of the cell. There was still so much to do, and her claw was throbbing from the constant pricking of the needle, but she went to sleep knowing that at least she had made a start.

If she thought that was the end of it, however, the end of the week held a rude surprise. More sacks. More ripped clothing from Procruste Ant Inc. Sewing, sewing, sewing! It was never ending, and it continued week in, week out, for months, but she always managed to complete the task before the deadline arrived. As she sewed, she dreamed of the day she'd be allowed to buzz around the garden and see the flowers once more. She received no guests. Not even her parents were permitted to visit, to her constant despair. There was one exception, however.

Every first day of the month, at precisely ten o'clock in the morning, the queen would pay a royal visit to Samantha's cell and inquire as to whether or not she still refused to acknowledge that her life rested in her royal claws. Samantha could sense that, like so many bees in the hive, what the queen wanted was to be told that she was right. She suspected that all she had to do was agree to what the queen said and she'd be set free.

Except, she couldn't, no matter how much she yearned to feel the wind in her face and the sunlight on her wings, or yearned to see her parents again.

She couldn't because the queen *wasn't* right. She couldn't betray her beliefs, and she certainly couldn't betray the Great Mother, even if it meant that she was locked away in this dingy cell for the rest of her life, locked away from her family and the things she loved. It was at these moments she'd recall the old actress in her dream: *To bee or not to bee*, which, she figured, meant being true to her beliefs.

So, like the question, the answer was always the same. "I believe only in the Way of the Goddess, the Great Mother Bee. My life rests in Her claws."

Queen Beetrix would then smile, and say, "We shall see, young lady, we shall see." And sometimes she would add: "Keep sewing!"

Ten times this had occurred, always the same, and always with Samantha confined within these cold, dark walls with nothing to keep her company except tatty pairs of underwear and overalls. If at all nothing else, she consoled herself, she was now a pretty accomplished seamstress. She had taught herself to double stitch, zigzag stitch, double zigzag stitch, spider stitch, blanket stitch, and loads more handy sewing techniques. She never thought she'd be so enthusiastic about such a menial task.

Sewing, however, was the last thing on her mind at that moment. Today was the anniversary of her imprisonment. It was also the first day of the month, and she sat on the bed waiting for the queen with a strange and uneasy feeling: today's encounter was going to be different than the previous occasions.

SHE DIDN'T HAVE long to wait. At precisely ten o'clock, she heard a rattle of keys outside the door. Samantha stood to greet her royal guest just as the lock was unbolted and two royal guards entered her tiny cell, each standing to one side. As was her duty, she curtseyed when the queen entered.

"Tell me if you're ready to answer my question," the queen said, summoning Samantha to rise. "Do you still refuse to believe that your life rests in my royal claws?"

To bee or not to bee, the old actress had said. "I believe only in the Way of the Goddess, the Great Mother Bee," Samantha said. "My life rests in Her claws."

Queen Beetrix Bee IV frowned, and then sighed rather loud and unroyal-like. "You have become thin and weak and your stinger is blunt," she said, and glanced Samantha up and down. "You've become this way because I have wished it to be. How can there be any doubt that it is I, not you, not anyone, who controls your life?"

To Samantha's surprise, the queen dismissed the guards with a curt wave. They objected at once, claiming it was too dangerous to leave Her Majesty alone with a prisoner. She hushed them and waited until they had shut the door on their way out.

"Every month I come to your cell and ask you the same question," she then said, "and every month you offer the same reply. To say the least, I am beginning to find it tiresome."

"That's because you don't understand the Great Mother's Way," Samantha said.

Queen Beetrix stared at Samantha blankly. Then she chuckled. "Young lady, you are certainly one of a kind. But I've not come to philosophize with you. I've come to tell you something." She paused, and

Samantha didn't like her smile. "I'm sending you to the Crazy Lands."

Samantha gulped and felt her wings suddenly stiffen. Fear rose into her heart from the cold floor like dank mist from a swamp. She glanced through the barred window to the distant hills, feeling more scared than the day she was sentenced to prison. No one had ever returned from the Crazy Lands in the living memory of the hive. She had heard that just a glimpse of one of the monsters that roamed there was enough to turn a bee into stone, and even if she were lucky enough to avoid them, then of course there was the wastelands. Miles and miles of barren desert littered with the withered exoskeletons of those unfortunates banished from the queendom. Nobody survived in the Crazy Lands for too long, and those that did went utterly, utterly mad. Up until now, she'd thought her life couldn't get any worse than it already had. How wrong could she be? This wasn't happening. This wasn't fair.

Just at that moment, a voice whispered through the window, carried, as it were, on the westerly wind. It was the same mysterious voice she'd heard a year ago, calling her into the rose.

"Samantha," it urged softly. "Be a bee."

She didn't know what to make of the voice. She glanced at the distant hills again, then back at the queen, who was still smiling as she had. "Things happen for a reason," Samantha said, holding her head high. "I am not afraid."

"Not now, perhaps," the queen said, "but you will be. You certainly will be." She went to the door, but just before she knocked for the guards to enter, she faced Samantha and said, as if an afterthought, "I'm in need of something, something that will earn you a pardon for your crimes. If it's accomplished to my

31

complete satisfaction, of course." Samantha pricked her antennae as the queen stepped toward her. Speaking in a low voice so as not to be overheard by the guards outside, she went on, "As you know, the High Priestess has complete control over the production of honey in the hive. It has to stop." She glanced at the door before continuing. "Have you heard of Beebylon?"

Samantha's antennae suddenly went rigid with astonishment. Every bee had grown up with the fable of Beebylon, the magical hive where dreams came true, where everyone was happy and no one ever got sick. It was said that in Beebylon honey dripped from the walls of the towering cliff on which it was built, that they had discovered honeyroot, the magical substance that turned stone into honey, the secret of Infinite Richness.

"The place in the fairytale, you mean?" she said.

Queen Beetrix Bee IV now stood tall, towering over Samantha, her demeanor as hard as the cell walls. "For your sake," she said, "you'd better start believing in fairytales. I want you to go to Beebylon and bring me honeyroot. Only then will I allow you to live with your mother and father again."

Samantha's hopes suddenly flew out between the bars of the window. The queen was asking the impossible, but what choice did she have? She could either stay here, rotting in this cell for the rest of her life, or she could risk everything and travel through the Crazy Lands in search of a fanciful dream. Crazy if she did. Crazy if she didn't.

She drew a deep breath and said, "You leave me no option. I'll find Beebylon and I'll bring back your honeyroot. Maybe then your eyes will open to the Way of the Great Mother."

The queen returned to the cell door. "Maybe, my child," she said, knocking for the guards to enter. "But you forget, I have nothing to lose out of this. You, on the other hand, have everything to lose. Including your sanity."

THAT AFTERNOON, SIX royal guards came to escort Samantha to the Crazy Lands. Her wings and legs shackled, they marched her out of the prison and through the hive gates, a guard on either side lifting her up beneath each wing. Samantha ignored the stares of the worker bees in the garden, averting her eyes elsewhere, barely able to believe that this was happening.

In the distance lay the forested hills. As she well knew, the Crazy Lands began miles before those undulating tors, at the brook where the wild roses grew. Halfway there, across the meadow of high grass, they came upon a large, crumpled wreck. It was diamond-shaped and made of some kind of red material she had never seen before. Two wooden crossbeams, broken and bent at awkward angles, were tethered together in the centre. A tangle of thread lay next to it. Only when she was directly above the wreckage did Samantha recognize it as the kite she'd seen from her prison window, the one that had crashed into the high grass exactly a year ago to the day. Then it was behind and out of sight.

It took another three hours before Samantha heard the babbling of shallow water. The crystal brook marked the end of the queen's realm and the beginning of the Crazy Lands. This was as far as any sane bee would go. The two guards carrying her put her down on the upper bank and removed her shackles.

"Enjoy your holiday!" the captain said, shoving her forward.

"And send me a postcard!" added another with a mocking laugh.

Samantha ignored them, not looking over her wings, not wanting to show the fear on her face. Like a scary book, the Crazy Lands opened up before her. Wild rose bushes grew to the side, and closer, just over the brook, a field of lush grass led up to a crop of sunflowers. The forested hills lay not too far in the distance, now much larger than before. The barren deserts littered with the bone-dried exoskeletons, she figured, must lay beyond the shimmering lake she could see in the valley. All in all though – and three happy cheers for small mercies – it didn't look that much different from the queen's realm.

The captain shoved her again and told her to get a move on. Samantha stumbled forward, then took a hesitant step toward the brook, and then another. Each step felt as if she was still walking with shackles, her feet seemingly hampered and joined together. The guards kept yelling at her to get a move on. At the water's edge, her wings began to flap and fret.

"Don't worry, Samantha," she said to herself. "Everything happens for a reason."

She closed her eyes, spread her stiff wings and buzzed into the air. After a year of confinement, flying was awkward and tiring at first. She struggled over the brook and into the Crazy Lands, with no particular thought in mind other than to seek refuge from the beasts and monsters that roamed these fields. With every flap of her wings, the taunts of the guards faded behind her, like the light of the setting sun.

Soon, she thought with dread, it would be dusk.

SAMANTHA HAD NEVER been alone at night outside the hive. At home she'd always been with her parents. Even in prison, although it had been dark and cold, there was always the security of knowing the four walls of the cell were protecting her from whatever lurked outside. Now though, in the vast open space of the Crazy Lands, she felt a knot of fear tighten inside, the first sign of panic.

At first it started as a faint queasiness. Then it began to squeeze her chest. She started to take quicker and shallower breaths, but this only made her head start to spin. Next, the fear stuck in her throat. She couldn't breathe. She tried to scream. It was the worse feeling she had ever had, as though she was drowning or suffocating, or both. She was certain she was going to die. She zipped through the air in one direction, then the other, up and down, forward and backward, buzzing in erratic and jerky circles like a maddened mosquito.

Then, like the kite she had once seen from her cell window, she began plummeting toward the ground, somehow forgetting how to fly. She couldn't tell which way was up or which way was down. With what could only be seconds before she crashed, she suddenly remembered her lessons at aerobatic flying school and quickly executed a blowfly back flip, a full reverse-loop with a half twist. For a brief moment she thought she'd managed to pull up and out of the dive, but as she came out of her half twist, she thumped into the belly of a sunflower. Unfortunately, it could only cushion the impact to a partial extent. Tumbling over, she felt her right wing bend and snap. The pain shot into her head, and she squealed in agony.

Dazed, she immediately tried to stand, but the pain caused her to cry out again. She slumped into a heap and tried to get up again. It did no good. Even the slightest movement made the pain flare. In the end, she decided to just rest and assess the situation.

The night was almost upon her, she saw. The stars were already twinkling and the moon had risen in the east. She figured she was safe where she was, high above the ground, and not too un-comfortable either, unless she moved. Despite the throbbing wing, she thought she'd be able to get through the night, maybe even sleep a little. To-morrow, when the sun had risen, she would see what she could do about it.

When sleep did finally come, it was fitful and dreamless. At one point she woke when something howled from the hills. It sounded far, but in the darkness it was difficult to tell. She then drifted back to sleep, stirring hours later to the twitter of a black-bird.

"Get up! Get up! Get up!" the bird sang. "The day is new. The sky is blue. Get up! Get up! Get up!"

A little confused as to where she was, she rolled over and was struck with a tearing stab of pain in her right wing. The flash of memory was just as sharp. She was in the Crazy Lands, and the queasy sensation of panic began to rise in her stomach once again; but unlike last evening, the pain helped to keep her emotions from bubbling out of control.

Cautiously, Samantha now got to her feet. The broken wing stabbed with pain again, but it soon settled into a bearable ache. One thing was for certain: she wasn't going to do much flying, not for a while, not until it mended. If she wanted to get to Beebylon and find the secret of turning stone into honey, she was going to have to start by walking. She looked around, wanting to get her bearings, to get orientated, as bees do when they rise. What she saw took her breath away.

In the field, meandering like a golden river toward the lake, thousands of sunflowers bathed in the soft morning light, thrusting their faces up to the sun in heavenly bliss. For a while she just soaked in the sight, letting her mind float in the peacefulness of it all. The Crazy Lands were nothing like she'd been told at all. In fact, it was nowhere near as bad as she'd feared.

Suddenly, from somewhere nearby, a booming holler shattered the dream. Samantha froze. It was undoubtedly one of the beasts that roamed these lands. If it saw her, she'd be turned to stone.

Then it hollered again. From directly below.

SAMANTHA DIDN'T KNOW what to do. She couldn't fly away. She couldn't run. Trapped on top of the sunflower, there was no place to hide.

The beast again hollered, though this time it had sounded less like a savage creature and more like the Hive Crier just before the gates were shut for the night. "Hear ye! Hear ye! Hear ye!"

Samantha decided to investigate, risking the very real danger of becoming a bee-statue for rest of eternity. She peered over the edge of the sun-flower to where she thought the sound was coming from. Annoyingly, leaves and shadows blocked her view of the ground. She would have to get closer. Taking care with her broken wing, she climbed down the stem to the ground. To her surprise, she saw a small gnat near the base of another sun-flower stem. He was rather plump, and he held a small stick like a walking cane. For some reason, he was standing on a soapbox on which was written one word:

JOY

He seemed delighted when Samantha stepped forward to hear him speak. "Hear ye! Hear ye! Hear ye!" he hollered, although no one else except Sam-antha was in the vicinity. "Step right up! Step right up!" he said, and tapped his cane on the soapbox three times. "You don't want to miss the show."

Stepping closer toward the soapbox, Samantha frowned and scratched her head, wondering what on earth he was talking about.

"I'm a gnat, to be exact, an' grammatical play is mar game," he said. He had an outrageous accent and, if she wasn't mistaken, his "I am" sounded a little like "arm." "A rhetoric or two, from me to you, an' never the noun the same."

Samantha smiled and waited for more. His words seemed to roll off his tongue in an amusing and jovial way. "I'm a will-o'-the-wisp, an' elusive as light. To those who know, I'm *Ignis Fatuus*, a sprite!" He said this with a laugh and a twinkle in his eyes. "I'm here, I'm there, so catch me if you dare. Once bitten, twice shy, the writer's bug am I."

He laughed and tapped his cane three times on the soapbox again. "One man's fish is another man's poison, just be careful when cooking the two. Some say *tomarto*, I say *tomayto*, but how does it sound to you?" He paused briefly, smiling as he had, before going on. "A verb, I dictate, is a predicate, but the subject is full of nouns. And pray, take heed, watch the objective of an adjective, or it'll run the show like a clown." Samantha clapped and the grammatical gnat bowed in appreciation. Then he stood erect and continued. "A verb and a noun will a sentence construct, but silence the blurb of a silly adverb or you'll begin to sound like a duck." He really was full of surprises. "The passive tense you must avoid, but can you avoid a void?"

Samantha stared back at him with a vacant expression. The gnat was grinning, still with a twinkle in his eyes. "A void is nothing, is it not?" he said, twirling his cane like a baton. "It exists because the opposite, something, does not. Nothing, therefore, is dependent on something. But is not the definition of nothing the non-existence of something?" Samantha scratched her head and the gnat chuckled. "It is quite logical, is it not, to declare that something is nothing and nothing is something?"

Samantha felt her mind go suddenly topsy-turvy. It seemed as though she couldn't avoid a void. "Oh, dear," she said. "My head is starting to spin."

The gnat continued to smile and twirl the cane. "The proper position of your apposition will help you avoid a void." He suddenly pointed to the heavens with his cane, and said, "Kite gliding!" Samantha looked up to the cloudless sky, but could see no gliding kite. "Do you see, mar dear? With the proper position of your apposition, you will always avoid a void."

Samantha nodded, though if she were totally honest with herself she really didn't have a clue as to what he meant.

"And what is your name, mar pretty gal?" ("Mar purdy gaaaal" was actually what he said.)

"Samantha B. Honeycomb," she said.

"Ah, Samantha, 'tis a beautiful name: a rose for a rose." He beamed a smile as wide as the golden river of sunflowers she had seen earlier from above. Magically, he reached behind her left antennae and conjured a miniature crimson rose on a long stem, then handed it to her.

Samantha accepted the tiny replica with delight. It was perfect in every detail, from the thorns to the petals to the leaves. She asked his name.

The gnat threw back his head and laughed and laughed and laughed, holding his plentiful belly. "Mar name, by fortune and fame, is none other than Gerald The Great. I am deeee-lighted to be at your service, ma-dam." He bowed extravagantly. "I used to be Gerald The Gorgeous," he said, now standing erect, "but mar wife has gone an' lef' me for another more gorgeous than I. I thought it was time a-proper to change mar name."

Samantha didn't know whether to laugh or cry, but because he was smiling, so did she. Gerald tapped his cane three more times and said, "Now, mar purdy gal, what brings you into this untamed land?"

Samantha told him of her banishment from the hive after spending a year in prison for breaking the ancient laws forbidding worker bees to enter the sacred heart of a rose. She also told him that the queen had offered her the chance to earn a pardon for her crimes, but that she was distraught because she feared she would never find the fabled hive of

Beebylon, and that she would never be able to see her mother and father again. She had also broken her wing. It was a disaster. She didn't know what to do.

Gerald nodded thoughtfully and slowly twirled his cane. "Mar li'l honeybee," he said, finally, "if I may be so bold as to say, it seems that your destiny is dependent upon one simple fact: whether or not you discover the true egg-zistence of a fable."

Samantha thought about it for a moment, a little confused. "What do you mean by destiny?"

"Your destiny is your Bee Dream. It is that point at which you can be the best you can ever bee," Gerald said, chuckling. "In your case, mar dear, Beebylon is your destiny, whether you find it or not."

To bee or not to bee, the old actress had said in her dream. Perhaps, Samantha thought, she had meant for her to seek out her destiny and be the best that she could bee. It sounded credible, though it was the first time she'd ever been told she was in possession of her own destiny, or Bee Dream, as Gerald The Great called it. In the hive, everyone's destiny was the same, pretty much, except now he was telling her otherwise. She believed that things happened for a reason, but did that actually mean things happened to help her fulfill her Bee Dream, her destiny?

It was certainly a lot to think about; and if it were true, there was just one small problem: she didn't know where to begin. She didn't even know in which direction to head. North, south, east or west, Beebylon could be anywhere. She now felt like one of the many dragonflies she had seen hovering over the goldfish pond near the hive, drifting this way and that, hither and thither, not knowing which way to go to next.

41

"Fortunately, the Great Mother will always help you in your search to bee your best," Gerald The Great said, somehow knowing what Samantha was thinking. "She speaks to every one of us in the *Universal Language* all creatures understand, and She gives us signs to follow so that we can fulfill our individual Bee Dream."

Samantha hadn't paid it much consideration till now, but wasn't it odd how she, a honeybee, could understand what gnats and blackbirds were saying, and vice versa? Though they were all different, they were somehow able to communicate with each another, as if every living creature spoke a common language. She didn't know how it was possible, but she would bet a vat of honey that it had something to do with the *Universal Language* Gerald The Great was talking about.

She also had a hunch she knew what he meant about signs from the Great Mother. Omens, her godmother had called them. She again recalled the river of golden sunflowers she'd seen when she'd woken. Bees adored flowers. Everyone knew that. Was the Great Mother using them to give direction, a sign to follow?

"I believe I'm meant to follow the sunflowers to the lake," she now said to Gerald The Great. "That's where I'll find my Bee Dream."

"And indeed you shall. Indeed you shall," Gerald The Great said, laughing and tapping his cane on the soapbox, "as long as you follow the simple rule a wise old ladybird once taught me." He cleared his throat, like an opera singer about to perform, and in a fine tenor voice, with his claw on his heart, began to sing.

Follow your joy
And you will know
The way the ri-ver floh-ows.

Follow your joy
And you will see
The best that you can be-e.

Follow your joy
And you will show
The light the rest can fol-low

Follow your joy
Follow you joy
Follow your joy-oy-oy

He sang this once more, then said with a kindly chuckle, "'Tis a noble quest to follow your path and be the best that you can bee. I wish you well."

To Samantha's sudden disappointment, Gerald The Great stepped off his soapbox on which was written JOY and made ready to leave. She pleaded with him to stay.

"I must go to wherever I'm called, mar li'l rose," he said, smiling. He put his claw to his ear, listening to the faint sound of something carried on the wind. "Ah, can you hear? Someone is calling mar name."

Samantha couldn't hear anything except the breeze through sunflower leaves and the grumble of her tummy.

"You've been a most attentive audience and I thank you." Gerald The Great took a bow and bade her farewell, but just as he was about to disappear from view he turned around and said, "Remember two things, Samantha. Firstly, the Great Mother is always trying to help you to bee your best. And secondly, if you don't know to which flower you wish to fly, then no wind is helpful." Then he turned and vanished behind a sunflower stem.

Samantha began to hum the tune that he had just taught her. She now had direction, a purpose: she needed to get to the lake and find Beebylon. She felt a deep joy at the thought of it, a feeling that welled up from deep down inside her. She cocked her head and held her claw to her ear like Gerald The Great. "Samantha! Come hither!" she heard on the westerly wind, ever so softly. "Samantha!"

It worked! It was as though the Great Mother was calling her from the lake! She laughed and clapped excitedly. The miniature crimson rose, she suddenly noticed, had vanished into thin air, like Gerald The Great. Perhaps it was another sign. If she didn't follow the omens, her Bee Dream would vanish too.

She began heading toward the lake, wondering if, just maybe, Beebylon was as wonderful and magical as it sounded.

SAMANTHA WAS KIND of glad to be walking in the cool shade of the sunflowers instead of flying above them in the direct heat of the sun. Not that she had a choice; it would be weeks before her wing was healed.

She pondered the reason why it had broken. She knew *how* it had happened, but the how and the why of things were two completely different vats of honey. It was quite easy to get the two mixed up. Breaking her wing was a simple case of cause and effect: she had collided with the sunflower (the

44

cause), and her wing had snapped (the effect). That wasn't *why* she had broken it, though. Only the Great Mother knew that at this particular moment, and although she didn't know the reason herself, Samantha was content to let it be. One day she would understand the why of it.

She plodded on for most of the morning, following the sunflowers toward the lake. She whiled away the time humming the Song of Joy, or just watching the blackbirds fly high overhead, or simply enjoying the freedom of walking. Since the encounter with Gerald The Great, her fear had greatly diminished. She more than suspected that the tales of the Crazy Lands were greatly exaggerated; she had seen no evidence to support the frightening accounts, no beast tracks in the dirt, no ravaged carcasses or flesh-picked exoskeletons. In fact, there didn't seem to be a lot of *anything* out here except sunflowers, and she began to wonder whether she would walk all day without meeting anyone else.

As the sun approached its peak, she began to tire, though decided to carry on a little bit further before looking for a place to rest. At that moment, she heard someone talking loudly to themselves up ahead, behind one of the sunflower stems. "One step, two steps, three steps, four, five steps, six steps, seven steps more."

Samantha hurried into a small clearing and saw an orange caterpillar running (or walking very quickly, Samantha couldn't tell) around and around a large white teapot with purple polka dots, counting her steps as she went. A ring of flattened grass encircled the pot, and, as with the soapbox on which Gerald The Great had delivered his fabulous sermon, something was inscribed on it:

Furthermore, not too far from the teapot was a colorless tube-like thing that Samantha hadn't a clue as to what it was. It was about the same size as the caterpillar, and wrinkly, very wrinkly, like some of the old drones her father knew. It was also extremely thin, as thin as the membrane of a bee wing.

"One step, two steps, three steps, four, five steps, six steps, seven steps more," the caterpillar said, over and over.

Samantha was dizzy just watching her. The caterpillar had so many feet and they moved so fast, she wasn't sure how she could keep count. Samantha wandered closer, watching and waiting to see if she could grab a moment to talk to her. The caterpillar completed another lap, and still Samantha waited. After another five minutes, it was becoming obvious she wouldn't get the opportunity she wanted; the caterpillar hadn't slowed, nor even looked as if she were going to.

"One step, two steps, three steps, four," said the caterpillar at the beginning of each lap, "five steps, six steps, seven steps more."

The caterpillar was so busy she probably didn't have the time to eat. "Excuse me, miss," Samantha said, but there was no response, not even a twitch of an antenna. She repeated herself, this time a little louder. Again there was no response. "*Excuse me!*" she shouted at the top of her voice.

The caterpillar stopped in her tracks, none too happy at having her routine interrupted. Scrutinizing Samantha up and down, unsure as what to make of her, she said, "Who and *what* might you be?"

Slightly embarrassed at the question, Samantha introduced herself, then added, "I'm a honeybee."

"I see," said the caterpillar, coming to examine Samantha a little closer. She was quite thorough too, feeling her all over like a nursery maid would inspect a newborn grub. Samantha stood still, thinking it rude not to let the caterpillar touch her. Maybe it was the way caterpillars communicated.

"We may look different, but I wouldn't say we're *that* dissimilar," the caterpillar said in a thoughtful tone, feeling Samantha's left antennae. Then she felt Samantha's head. "We both have exoskeletons to protect us, though mine isn't as hard as yours, and we both have antennae to detect vibrations and eyes to see," she said, speaking more to herself than to Samantha. "We also have limbs to move about and to pick things up with, except I have fourteen and you have six." She then moved around to examine Samantha's back. "Do all honeybees have these?" she asked, and grabbed Samantha's broken wing.

Samantha yelped in pain, and the caterpillar stepped back, apologizing. Her name was Lizzie McCoon, she informed Samantha, returning to the teapot. She had seen enough. "It was nice to meet you, Miss Honeycomb, but I don't have the time for idle chitchat, if that's what you want. I'm a very busy woman," she said. "I'm in the middle of something extremely important."

"What exactly are you doing?" Samantha asked.

"Isn't it obvious? I'm counting. Watch and learn!" Lizzie then circled the base of the teapot, chanting, "One step, two steps, three steps, four," eventually stopping one hundred and two steps later. "See. It's easy."

Samantha scratched her head. "You do it very well, but why do you do it all?"

Lizzie just stared. "That's what caterpillars *do*," she said. "Besides, it keeps me busy. So if you'll excuse me, I have business to attend to."

Lizzie returned to her hectic schedule without further ado, running and running in circles, around and around and around. Samantha considered what Lizzie had said and wasn't at all convinced that counting steps was what caterpillars were meant to do. "I thought caterpillars made cocoons," she said, when Lizzie completed another lap.

Lizzie suddenly stopped and eyed her with contempt. "What do you take me for, a maggot?" Samantha shook her head until she felt dizzy, wondering how on earth she'd managed to offend the orange caterpillar. "Well, good. Moths make cocoons. I, like all butterfly progeny, make chrysalises." She was thoughtful for a moment. "But we only do that when we want to complete our metamorphosis, you know."

"I know exactly what you mean," Samantha said, jumping at the chance to make up for her recent offence. "I went through the very same thing when I was a grub. I didn't become a beautiful butterfly, though, just an ordinary honeybee."

"You did?" Lizzie asked, her eyes growing wide. "What was it like?"

"The pupation stage, you mean?" Samantha drew a breath and puffed her cheeks. "Well, I must say it was pretty frightening at first. My muscles and nerves and everything else dissolved, which kind of felt like I was melting away." She saw Lizzie's eyes widening even more. Her exoskeleton suddenly paled from orange to grey-brown, like faded autumn leaves. "But my new muscles and nerves formed almost immediately," she quickly added. "It sounds worse than it actually is. In fact, if I didn't go through it, I wouldn't have grown wings. I would never have known the joy of flying."

Lizzie's eyes were still wide and her color had yet to return to normal. "Flying? Hmm, well, I think I'll stick to walking. I like counting my steps. It's what caterpillars do."

"But don't you want to make a chrysalis?" asked Samantha.

"It's not that simple, you know," the caterpillar said. "The right conditions have to be met. I can't just do it anywhere, you know. Besides, I'm secure and happy with what I do. I don't see any reason to change."

Once again Samantha glanced at the flattened ring around the teapot, thinking of Gerald The Great and what he had told her. "Because only when we follow the Great Mother's signs to our destiny can we ever be the best that we can bee," she said. "Our destiny's our Bee Dream. Everything happens in our life to guide us to it."

Lizzie cocked an antenna, briefly lost in thought. "You know, maybe you're onto something. I have always wanted to make the most beautiful chrysalis in the world. If it's possible for a caterpillar to have a Bee Dream, maybe that's it." Then she sighed. "But I've never got around to doing anything about it. I'm so busy counting steps, I don't have the time."

"It's never too late to start," Samantha said, and told Lizzie how she had only just embarked on her quest to find honeyroot, the secret to Infinite Richness. Until recently, she was just another honeybee living in the colony, not doing much other than collecting nectar like everyone else, just trying to survive. She was now following the river of golden sunflowers to the lake in the hills and Beebylon, her Bee Dream. "I believe that everything happens for a reason," she said, and then sang Lizzie the Song of Joy Gerald The Great had taught her.

Lizzie wanted another minute to think about it, and commenced yet another lap around the teapot. "One step, two steps, three steps, four, five steps, six steps, seven steps more." When she returned, she was smiling. "I've thought about what you've said, Samantha Honeycomb," Lizzie said, "and if it's agreeable with you, I should like to accompany you on your quest to find your Bee Dream. If Beebylon is as magical as you say, maybe that's where I can also find the right conditions to make my chrysalis."

Samantha smiled. "Reet Bee-teet!" she said, and then saw that Lizzie looked a little confused. She explained that Reet Bee-teet was bee-slang for "all right."

"Reet Bee-teet it is then," Lizzie said, flush with color. "Now, which way do we go?"

SAMANTHA SHOWED LIZZIE the direction that they should head with a little six-step bee dance. She jigged and jived in a figure 8, which the bees in the hive used to tell other bees the direction of a new source of nectar. She was now doing the same thing, only they weren't going to gather nectar, they were going to find Beebylon and their Bee Dream. She repeated the dance a few times, waiting until Lizzie understood where to go.

Soon thereafter, they headed off. They wandered westward through the undergrowth at a leisurely pace, weaving in and around the tall sunflower stems, over tumbled petals and leaves, beneath the occasional fallen flower (which seemed to always make Samantha feel sad) and on towards the lake nestled between the forested hills.

"We've walked two thousand, six hundred and ninety-three steps since we began our quest," said Lizzie a little later. She was looking awfully pleased with her work to date. "Quite a long way."

Samantha felt compelled to congratulate her new friend, also pleased, for that meant they were two thousand, six hundred and ninety-three steps closer to their destination. Unfortunately, it also meant that they were that much further away from the hive and her parents. It seemed ironic that the closer she got to her Bee Dream, the more distant she was from the ones she loved. She tried not to think about it for too long; it only made the journey harder. Instead, she concentrated on what she had to do at this moment, which was walk. If she brooded over the past, she wouldn't get anywhere, and what was the point in that? The only way was forward.

At that moment, Samantha heard the snapping of a twig. Lizzie had heard it too. They spun around to where the noise was coming from, but there seemed to be nobody there, only sunflower stems. Oddly, Samantha could also sense the faint aroma of musk. They looked at each other and shrugged, agreeing that it was probably nothing more than a leaf falling to the ground, or something similar.

Without further ado, they continued on their way. Samantha told Lizzie about how she came to be in the Crazy Lands. She described in detail her trial and imprisonment, the long days spent sewing and patching overalls and underwear from Procruste Ant Incorporated (Lizzie hadn't heard of it either,

51

when asked), the monthly visits by Queen Beetrix Bee IV, and her exile from the queendom. When she mentioned the crimson rose and explained the ancient laws forbidding worker bees to enter its corolla, Lizzie was amazed.

"Why do you have laws that stop you being a bee?" she asked.

"I think," Samantha said, who had spent a lot of the time in prison mulling over this very question, "that whoever made the laws thought there was not enough honey for everyone, so they tried to protect it."

As she pondered on the logic of the ancient lawmakers, she considered the sunflowers towering above her. Because they were growing so close to each other, they had grown exceedingly tall and straight. Competition for sunlight was encouraging them to grow faster and faster, each outreaching the other, higher and higher, for no other purpose, it seemed, than to outdo the closest neighbor. It was as though the sunflowers believed there was not enough sunlight for all of them, and only the tallest and straightest of them would survive.

Life in the hive reminded her of the sunflowers. The bees were in constant competition with one another, always striving to outdo their neighbor or co-worker. The High Priestess had duped them into believing there was not enough honey to go around. Yet, no matter how much they had, many bees weren't happy. "Honey is always sweeter in the other jar," as the saying went, and while they continued their westward trek, she hummed a song the worker bees sang in the fields:

Honey and you and me make three,
Honey on our bread,
    And honey in our tea.
Honey makes the life of
    A little honeybee.

Later, they stopped for a lunch at the base of a rather shady sunflower. According to Lizzie, they had walked seven thousand, eight hundred and twelve steps without a break. It was a good day's work so far, and they deserved a little snack. Lizzie found a juicy leaf but said she would only eat half because caterpillars had their main meal at night. Besides, she added, she was trying to go on a diet. She held out a portion of the leaf for Samantha to taste.

"Go on, why don't you give it a try?" Lizzie said. "If you're worried about your figure, there's only twenty-six calories per leaf."

Samantha wasn't actually too concerned about her figure at all. In fact, it was probably the furthest thing from her mind at this particular moment. She politely refused Lizzie's offer. She wanted to climb to the top of the nearest sunflower and find some nectar.

Lizzie's antennae stiffened with horror; and for a fleeting, ghastly moment, Samantha thought she'd seen a human. "You can't just eat nectar all the time," Lizzie said. "Do you know how many calories there are in that stuff?" Samantha shrugged, and Lizzie added, "I can see I'm going to have to keep an eye on your diet. It's a good job I came along with you."

For two days they traveled, forever westward, following a simple routine of rising early, napping after lunch, and retiring with the nightlight of the moon. On the third morning of her journey through the Crazy Lands, Samantha stirred from a peaceful slumber, rubbed her antennae and sat upright. Her right wing still felt sore, but it was infinitely better. Lizzie was curled into a ball next to her, mumbling in her dreams: "One step, two steps, three steps, four, five steps, six steps, seven steps more."

Samantha stepped out from under the leaf they were using as shelter and craned her neck. It was a beautiful morning, the kind of morning she would often buzz around the gardens in the queendom admiring the roses and geraniums and tulips, not the kind of morning she ever imagined could exist in the Crazy Lands. She heard a blackbird twitter its morning song: "Get up! Get up! Get up! The day is new. The sky is blue. Get up! Get up! Get up!"

While Lizzie slept, Samantha climbed to the top of the nearest sunflower to gaze upon the distant lake. On the western horizon, between the forested hills, the blue waters reminded her of a meadow of hyacinths, or delphiniums, and the sunflower field of a stream of golden rays from the morning sun. The sight never ceased to render her speechless. Even if Beebylon was just a myth, and her efforts to find her Bee Dream were all in vain, at least she'd seen the beauty of the lake and the sunflowers.

When she returned to the base of the stem, Lizzie had risen and was already eating breakfast. Lizzie offered her the remains of what was until very recently their makeshift shelter, stressing the importance of a diet high in fiber. What's more, it only had twenty-six calories, if she didn't already know.

Samantha courteously demurred. After performing the figure 8 dance to show Lizzie the direction of the lake, she began to lead the way again. Although she enjoyed Lizzie's company, it was frustrating walking at such a slow pace. She felt as though an invisible force was deliberately holding her back, keeping her from getting to the lake. If her wing hadn't broken, she could have buzzed straight there and reached her destiny by now. Alas, it wasn't to be.

Samantha was suddenly distracted from her flow of thoughts. She had heard a noise up ahead, like a hiss, or a harsh whisper. That wasn't all. She'd also caught a whiff of something unpleasant and musky. Lizzie sensed it too. Samantha glanced back to where she thought she'd heard the noise and saw a face peeking behind a dead leaf, as black as the stripes on a honeybee. It also had antennae, which it wiggled. Then, in a flash, it was gone.

"What was that?" Lizzie asked, making a grab for Samantha. "I didn't like the look of it at all."

Samantha gently removed Lizzie's claw from her arm. "I think it was an army ant," she said, and then wandered over to the dead leaf. The smell of musk hung thicker here, and there were many tracks in the soil. Her eyes followed to where they disappeared into the forest of sunflower stems. At least three or four army ants, she guessed, had been spying on them.

Feeling uncomfortable with the thought of being watched, she continued on, making a wide detour around the tracks. She said no more to Lizzie for a while. It was best not to mention that the ants had scampered away exactly in the direction where they wanted to go.

Toward the lake.

ABOUT TWO THOUSAND, two hundred and fifty paces onward, Samantha noticed a red-green dragonfly hovering above a sunflower. She told Lizzie that they must be near a water source, a pond or a river. It seemed the dragonfly was just drifting, this way and that, not particularly worried which way it went. She watched it for a little while, wishing that she could fly again. Though, she mused, she wouldn't just drift. She had a destiny to reach.

If you don't know to which flower you wish to fly, then no wind is helpful, Gerald The Great had said.

All of a sudden, a whirling gust of wind blew the dragonfly out of sight. Samantha glanced upward and was startled to see dark clouds blowing in from the east. Hopefully, she and Lizzie would get lucky. The front might blow past or blow itself out. There was something else too, though, something untoward she kept to herself: the smell of musk carried on the wind.

They then stepped into a small clearing and came upon an unusual item, a large playing card leaning against a sunflower stem. It towered above them, like the face of a cliff. "The Queen of Hearts," Samantha said. It had probably been blown there by the gusty wind. "I wonder what it means."

"It doesn't mean anything," Lizzie said, craning her neck. "It's just an extraordinarily large playing card."

Samantha thought otherwise. It was an omen: the Queen of Hearts represented love. She told her friend that perhaps that was what they'd discover at the lake.

Lizzie spun around. "Do you really think so?" she asked, just as a gust of breeze whipped past and shook the sunflowers. The card teetered, and then toppled over. She and Samantha jumped out of the way, narrowly avoiding being squashed. On the reverse side, staring up at them, was a word:

ACCEPTANCE

What did love have to do with acceptance? Samantha thought. It was just one more oddity she'd encountered in the Crazy Lands, starting with Gerald The Great's soapbox with the word JOY, then Lizzie's teapot with SECURITY, and now this, the Queen of Hearts with her message of ACCEPTANCE.

"If I were a playing card, I would probably be the lonely two of spades, the card that nobody wants," Lizzie said, sighing. She looked at Samantha with a hopeful, almost desperate, plea in her eyes. "D'you think it's at all possible to change the card you are?"

Samantha shrugged, and said, "What if you were the whole deck, not just one card?"

A curious glint came to Lizzie's eyes. "Then I'd choose whatever card I wanted to be," she said. "Sometimes I'd choose to be a king, and sometimes a jack, even a number, like the eight of diamonds, or even the two of clubs. I guess it'd depend on how I felt at the time." Lizzie took another moment to consider what she wanted to be. "Today I feel like the Queen of Hearts," she said, smiling. "Because now everyone we meet will love me."

"Then I'll be the King of Hearts," Samantha said, waving her clenched claw high above her head and pretending to brandish a weapon, "because we're on a quest and we need a brave heart and a mighty sword to fight the good fight."

They went on with renewed hope in their hearts, deeper into the uncharted terrain of the Crazy Lands. For the most part they kept to themselves, content to walk in silence. Samantha climbed to the top of a sunflower after lunch to make sure they were still heading in the right direction. The breeze was strong at the top. Behind, from the east, the faces of the sunflowers were all bending toward her, as if she were the setting sun, and her initial hopes that she and Lizzie might be able to avoid the storm quickly disappeared.

Before she headed back down, a glint of sunlight caught her attention. She looked closer. As she had suspected earlier, there was a water source nearby. Although some sunflowers partially obstructed her view, she could easily see a stream flowing toward the lake along the northern edge of the sunflower field. At first glance it was wider and deeper than the brook she had crossed from the queendom into the Crazy Lands. The brook was probably a tributary of this stream, and a sudden idea filled her with optimism. What if she and Lizzie were to float down the stream to the lake? It would surely be quicker than walking. They would have to sit on something that floated, of course, like a felled sunflower. If they wanted to make it sturdier, they could probably lash two or three sunflower stems together with some twine, something like she had seen with the crossbeams of the wrecked kite. Lizzie could help. She was a caterpillar. Maybe she could spin some super-strength silk for the twine. It would be easy.

Samantha hurried back down and told Lizzie of her plan for floating down the stream.

"It's a silly idea," Lizzie said. "I can't swim. What if I fell overboard? I'd drown."

Samantha lowered her head. At the rate they were traveling it would take weeks, if not months, to get to the lake. She wasn't going to argue with her friend, however. She danced a figure 8, a little slower and with less enthusiasm than before, and headed off. Neither she nor Lizzie said a word for quite a while, not until the storm hit that afternoon.

It didn't rain, but it blew and blew and blew. Though they'd been expecting it for some while, it struck so fast that Samantha and Lizzie were taken by surprise. Dust and leaves blew past them, even the large playing card they'd seen earlier. It tumbled end over end, almost hitting Samantha before the wind picked it up and flung it over the tops of the sunflowers and out of sight. Samantha and Lizzie, themselves, were almost blown off their feet.

"We need shelter!" Lizzie yelled. Though close by, her voice was almost lost in the gale.

Suddenly, the wind uprooted a sunflower not too far from them. It was almost picked up and flung in the direction of the Queen of Hearts. Instead, it wobbled and crashed into the earth, its head snapping clean off.

Samantha had an idea. She shouted for Lizzie to follow. Bracing against the wind, she scampered to the stem and clung desperately to it with all her strength. Lizzie, however, was struggling to make it over. She stretched out her claw for Samantha to take. Samantha snatched at it, but a huge gust of wind picked Lizzie up off her feet and blew her backwards. Fear flashed in her wide eyes. Then she instinctively curled herself into a ball and was sent tumbling out of sight.

"Lizzie!" Samantha screamed.

There was no answer.

The wind blew even stronger, rushing past like a stampeding herd. Samantha screamed again for Lizzie. The sound of her voice was immediately trampled, and once again there was no answer from her friend. Samantha knew that she had two choices: stay clinging to the sunflower stem and lose her friend forever, or let go and let the wind take her where it had taken Lizzie.

It took less than a second to decide. The instant Samantha released her grip on the stem, the wind plucked her off the ground and tossed her into the air. She yelped in fright, flying backwards, tumbling head over stinger, over and over for quite some time. Then abruptly, she thudded into something hard, something that felt much harder than the stem of a sunflower. The air was forced out of her and the spine of her good wing snapped like the other had done. The pain was intense, and with no breath to cry out she slumped to the ground, enveloped in blackness.

She knew not how long she lay unconscious. It could have been hours, or even days, and when she stirred the air was deathly still, not even the slightest breath of breeze. Oddly, the light was very bright. She heard some footsteps and whispers nearby, then a shadow fell across her line of sight. To her horror, she caught a whiff of musk.

She tried to call out for Lizzie, but her voice was choked with fear. The shadow loomed large and the musk wafted stronger.

Then she blacked out again.

PART TWO

IT WASN'T THE pain of her broken wings that roused Samantha from her semi-coma, but the singing. It echoed into the bright white chamber in which she found herself like an army platoon chanting the same song over and over as they marched down a tunnel.

> *This is my needle!*
> > *This is my thread!*
> *This is the work that earns our bread!*
> *Left, right, left, right.*
>
> *One for the sunshine!*
> > *One for the snow!*
> *This is the way we patch and sew!*
> *Left, right, left, right.*

With discomfort, Samantha propped herself into a sitting position upon the bed she was lying. She suddenly heard a familiar and welcome voice.

"Samantha! I thought you were never going to wake up. You've been out for almost a day."

Lizzie was on an adjacent bed with some of her legs wrapped in bandages. She got up and hobbled over to sit next to Samantha. "I've dislocated three legs and I'm a bit battered and bruised. And I see they've also put your wings in plaster."

Still slowly coming around, Samantha surveyed her new surroundings. The whitewashed room was as small as the cell in Hive Prison. Though where that room had been smelly and cold, this one was positively sterile. It even smelled of disinfectant.

There were sheets on the bed, too, crisp and heavy with starch. At the end of the bed was what appeared to be a neatly folded pair of denim overalls, something that seemed completely out of place.

"Do you remember what happened?" she asked Lizzie.

"Not much, only that we're extremely fortunate those ants were there to save us. We survived a terrible disaster."

Lizzie then related what she could recall. Lizzie had been blown into a camp of army ants many, many miles downwind. At first she'd been frightened, but the ants had taken care of her in the makeshift hospital. Though she was well nursed, she fretted over Samantha, thinking she'd never see her again, or worse, that she'd been killed in the storm. Thankfully, later that night, several ants brought Samantha to the hospital. They'd found her slumped at the base of a pine tree, not too far from the campsite. She was unconscious, but at least she was alive. The next morning, the ants carried Samantha and Lizzie on their backs to where they were now, in an ant hospital, underground. The doctors set Samantha's broken wings in plaster and said that they would be returning to check on her progress.

So they were underground, Samantha mused. That's why there were no windows. "I guess we should thank them for their hospitality," she said, trying to look at her plastered wings.

"There's no need for that," someone said, her voice cheery and melodic. "It's always a pleasure to treat strangers."

Samantha turned to see who'd spoken. An ant in a pair of denim overalls stood at the door with a stethoscope around her neck. Around her waist was a belt, on which were numerous small bottles filled with colored liquid – orange, crimson, purple, green – more colors than the rainbow, in fact. The ant introduced herself as Dr. 1754325Z. She then removed one of the bottles from her belt and sprayed a fine mist into the air. The perfume was like roses. Rather proudly, she showed Samantha and Lizzie the bottle. It was personally engraved with her name.

Wincing in discomfort, Samantha stood to greet her. Bemusedly, Dr. 1754325Z bent slightly forward and rubbed Samantha's antennae with her own, a customary greeting, the doctor explained, along with spraying something nice and welcoming. "I am already acquainted with your companion, Lizzie Mc-Coon," she said, attaching the bottled perfume back to her belt. "I hope you're feeling better."

Samantha thanked the doctor. She was still a bit under the weather and her wings still ached, but she was pleased to add that she was getting better with each moment that passed. She was confident that it wouldn't be long before she and Lizzie would be fit enough to embark on their travels once again. Curiously, she then saw Lizzie and the doctor share brief, but awkward glances.

"I've spoken with our glorious leader, the magnificent Procruste Ant," the doctor said, "and he's asked me to extend our fullest hospitality and spare you no courtesy."

Samantha stared at the ant, momentarily taken aback. The leader's name was the same as the tags on the overalls she had been forced to mend during her imprisonment.

"We have arranged some temporary accommodation for you in sector AX-49," the doctor continued. "You are most welcome to join us in the Procruste

Ant Incorporated Great Hall for dinner tonight. You have arrived at a very special time. Tonight is the last and biggest celebration of the Silly Season, when we celebrate our glorious leader's birthday. I am sure you must be very hungry after your ordeal, if nothing else."

Samantha looked over her plastered wings at Lizzie, who just shrugged. "Why not?" Samantha said to the doctor. "It's the least we can do to show our appreciation."

Pleased with what she'd heard, the doctor then instructed Lizzie and Samantha on the formalities of the dinner. Eveningwear was essential, and they could find a pair of overalls on the end of their beds. "We like to think of ourselves as an evolved species," she said. "We're not like all the other bugs in the insect world, you know. We're vastly superior. We have an advanced technological society. That's why we wear clothes."

Though they had been expertly tailored to fit the contours of their differing anatomies, the overalls were difficult to get into. Lizzie, at first, put hers on back to front and tripped when one of her legs got stuck. Samantha went over to help, glancing at the label while she did: PRODUCT OF PROCRUSTE ANT INC. There was a gap where the ONE SIZE FITS ALL had been neatly spliced out. "They obviously didn't expect bees or caterpillars for company," she said to herself. Her own pair felt awkward, especially with her broken wings. Never having worn clothes before, let alone overalls, the material felt scratchy and heavy, but once the initial discomfort passed, they were surprisingly easy to wear.

Once suitably dressed, Samantha and Lizzie were ushered to their new chambers in sector AX-49. To Samantha's surprise, two army guards with long, pointed spears accompanied them and Dr. 1754325Z. Just a routine precaution they took with foreigners, the doctor explained. Samantha thought their behavior a trifle overprotective; it felt too much like the royal guards escorting her to the courthouse. Lizzie, she also noticed, walked with her eyes to the ground, avoiding her gaze, and softly counted her steps.

They were led down many twisting corridors, left, right, up, down, all brightly lit by shimmering tubes on the ceiling (like stretched out glow worms, she reckoned) and smelling of disinfectant. On the walls were numerous portraits of an aging ant in a white coat and golden overalls. Wild strands of grey hair sprouted from the side of his balding, black head, and beneath his bulbous red nose was a proud, bushy, grey moustache. Around his neck was a red and gold bowtie, shaped like a daisy. Samantha wearily joked to Lizzie that the tie would most likely squirt water in her face if she stepped too close.

"That's our magnificent leader, the splendiferous Procruste Ant," the doctor said, as Samantha stared at one of the more garish images along the corridor. "Isn't he just *wonderful*?"

As they went, the soldierly chanting continued, echoing off the whitewashed walls:

> We are the ants that mend your pants!
> Left, right, left, right.
> We never say never,
>   And we never say can't!
>
> Left, right, left, right!
> Whether we sleep,
>   Or whether we fight,
> We sew all day and we sew all night!

Along they marched, seemingly in step with the rhythm of the songs, and eventually into their new lodgings. "We have just walked one thousand, six hundred and seventy-one steps in this underground maze," Lizzie said. "I'm not sure I could walk much further with my legs the way they are."

"That's the difference between caterpillars and ants," Dr. 1754325Z said. "We're vastly superior."

She then instructed her guests to be ready at 1900 hours for dinner. Procruste Ant simply did not tolerate tardiness. She fare-welled, briefly rubbing Lizzie and Samantha's antennae and spraying a rather pleasant perfume in the air, a mix of lavender and rosemary. When the doctor closed the door, Samantha heard a key turning in the lock, once again reminded of her time in Hive Prison.

"I'm exhausted," Lizzie said, scratching her face. "And I also have a funny craving for asparagus."

Samantha watched her hobble to one of the beds and flop down onto it. The room was identical to the one they had just left, except for one small detail. In the far corner, opposite the two beds, stood a wooden contraption. It had a large wheel and arms and things, even an inbuilt stool. She tried to guess its function, then looked back at the door.

"Is it me, or do you also get the feeling we're being held prisoner?" she asked. Lizzie averted her eyes, suddenly quiet. "Why do we need guards? Why have they locked the door? It's not exactly the sort of hospitality I'd bestow on my guests."

"I think ants are a little more cautious than bees," Lizzie said. "Perhaps they have to know you better before they let you wander through their nest."

Samantha let her remark pass, but there was something odd with the look in her eyes that suggested Lizzie knew more than she was letting on.

SAMANTHA AND LIZZIE were woken from their siesta by the jingle of keys in the lock at precisely 1900 hours. Flanked by two guards, they were marched down many twisting corridors, then finally through an imposing arched doorway and into the Procruste Ant Incorporated Great Hall. Samantha's antennae went rigid with amazement.

The hall was a spacious chamber filled with rows and rows of benches and tables set for a banquet. Seated at the tables were innumerable ants, all dressed in neatly pressed overalls and murmuring polite greetings to one another, rubbing antennae and spraying perfume. An ornate ceiling domed the hall, and suspended from its central beam was an extravagant chandelier. Encircling the Procruste Ant Inc. Great Hall, guards with pointed spears stood shoulder to shoulder against the walls, which were covered with red and gold drapes of the finest silk. Samantha had only seen such lavishness in the cathedral of the High Priestess Bee.

Furthermore, on a raised dais at the back of the hall stood a single table, larger and more imposing than the rest, made from a rich dark timber. Behind it were five empty chairs, the central one an elaborate, gilded throne. Four guards in black armor at the back of the dais stood motionless in front of an enormous portrait of the magnificent Procruste Ant that almost touched the dome ceiling. To one side of it stood a pine tree (it must have been a branch), decorated in strips of red and gold tinsel. A golden star topped the tree, and around its base was a neat stack of presents.

"We have a very similar celebration in the hive," Samantha whispered to Lizzie. "We call it the Great Mother Day and we give presents to each other as a symbol of the Great Mother's gift of life to us."

Samantha and Lizzie were ushered to the far side of the hall, where they were shown to two vacant places at the head of a table. Samantha and Lizzie self-consciously sat down, aware that all eyes in the room were upon them. The guards that had escorted them then left to stand sentry at the entrance. Sitting next to Samantha was Dr. 17543-25Z. She nodded and smiled welcomingly, spraying some rose scented perfume in the air. She leaned forward to rub their antennae.

"The ceremony's about to begin," the doctor said, whispering. "It's so exciting!"

Caught up in the moment, Samantha also told the doctor about the celebration of the Great Mother Day in the hive. Dr. 1754325Z's antennae suddenly went stiff and her black skin turned horridly grey. She glanced from side to side, looking at the guards lining the walls. "Samantha, shh!" she said, barely audible. "It's forbidden to mention the Great Mother. If any of the guards hear you speaking Her name, you'll be sentenced to death. Please, say no more."

The doctor then sat back and was silent. The minutes passed, and Samantha and Lizzie looked awkwardly around the hall, unsure how to behave. Thick silence of anticipation floated around the chamber like pollen in spring. Suddenly, trumpets blared from a dozen guards flanking the dais. Four beautiful female ants dressed in golden overalls, their shoulders draped in red silk shawls, walked onto the dais from the far side and sat on either side of the throne at the royal table.

Palpable expectation spread around the hall, building in strength with every passing second. Dr. 1754325Z and the others at the table trembled with excitement, as did every other ant that Samantha could see. No one spoke a word. No one sprayed perfume. The tension seemed to press against the very walls and ceiling.

Then the trumpets blared again. Onto the dais walked Procruste Ant to thunderous cheers and delirious screaming. Feet stamped on the floorboards. Mugs banged onto the tabletops. Clenched claws pumped toward the ceiling. The whole room was shaking.

"PROCRUSTE! PROCRUSTE! PROCRUSTE!" the ants chanted.

Every ant began spraying perfume into the air. It was like a heavy mist, scented with a hundred different aromas, rose, lavender, vanilla, rosemary, coconut, and many more. Halfway down the table, an ant fainted and slumped to the floor. Procruste nodded to two security guards, who rushed over and carried her away. The noise was deafening.

"PROCRUSTE! PROCRUSTE! PROCRUSTE!"

He stood at the front of the dais dressed in a white coat and golden overalls with a daisy-bowtie. Just like his portraits, he had a bulbous red orb for a nose, a bushy moustache and a wild tangle of grey hair at the side of his balding scalp. And there was another oddity Samantha noticed: his shoes were bright red and at least three times too big.

"Isn't he *marvelous*?" the doctor shouted.

For several minutes Procruste Ant held his arms outstretched, absorbing the praise. Unabated, the crowd continued to chant and stamp and punch the air. "PROCRUSTE! PROCRUSTE! PROCRUSTE!"

Then, just as Samantha thought the hall would collapse around her wings, Procruste gestured for silence. Immediately, the din stopped and the Great Hall was once again a theatre of expectant silence. He let the crowd wait a few more moments before speaking. Finally, like thunder, his voice boomed through the chamber.

"$E=MC^2$!"

The ants roared and punched the air, spraying lots of perfume.

Then the splendiferous leader gestured for calm again, waiting for complete silence. It took quite some time. "For every action there is an equal and opposite reaction!" he said.

The ants squealed and chanted his name with delight. The mist of perfume was now a fragrant cloud. Another ant fainted to Samantha's left, again efficiently whisked away by the security guards.

Procruste Ant held his clenched claw above his head, waiting again for silence. "A body in motion continues in a straight line unless acted upon by a force!"

The crowd was now in a frenzy of ecstasy. An ant tried to throw himself on the dais at Procruste's large feet, but he was caught and escorted out of the hall before anyone knew what had happened. (Samantha later learned that he was sentenced without trial to the salt mines for life.) Procruste glared across the hall, his claw still raised, and his voice boomed out: "Science is God!"

"SCIENCE IS GOD! SCIENCE IS GOD!" the ants chanted. Like a drop of icy water, a chill slid down Samantha's wings all the way to her stinger. "HAIL THE PROPHET PROCRUSTE! LONG LIVE THE PROPHET PROCRUSTE!"

The ants stamped their feet and punched the air, spraying perfume and screaming wildly. Several minutes later, and several more arrests, the hall settled and the ants took their seats. Then the courses were served, gastronomic delicacies from the four corners of the known world. Samantha stared at the food, ravenous. It had been many, many months since she had feasted on such a meal.

"Why don't you try some of this fruit pudding? It's delicious," she said to Lizzie, who had asked the waiters simply for a cabbage leaf and a stalk of asparagus.

"No, I simply couldn't," Lizzie said, staring at the pile of food on the plate. "Too many calories."

Samantha wondered why she was so afraid of putting on weight. To her limited but serviceable knowledge, caterpillars needed to get fat to survive the period of fasting during pupation. Samantha let it be, and began tucking into her delightful meal.

The celebrations continued on. The ants drank copious amounts of an intoxicating beverage they called *antwine*, and to raucous delight a six-piece jazz band began to play. The volume in the hall increased to the levels only previously matched by the maddening chants of "Science is God!" But it was a disorderly din. Hither and thither fights broke out around the hall. At one point, on the far side, fifty or more ants became involved in a brawl that had to be cordoned off by the guards to prevent it from spilling into the rest of the crowd. The guards simply waited until most had beaten themselves senseless and then dragged them out of the hall, to where Samantha didn't know. Procruste ate at the royal table with his wives, watching the events with a muted expression, and the band played on.

The wildness soon spread to Dr. 1754325Z and the other ants sitting nearby. A drunken ant vomited on the tomato salad and tortilla dips, and someone threw a bagel at his head. Within seconds a food fight erupted, during which the drunken ant passed out into his vegetable soup, then slumped to the floor. No one bothered to offer any assistance, and the band played on.

"Isn't this fun?" Dr. 1754325Z shouted above the hubbub. "I just *love* the Silly Season!" She swayed over to another drunken ant (another doctor whom Samantha and Lizzie had been introduced to as Dr. 5689214G) and sat in his lap, giggling like a little grub. After a while, arm in arm, they staggered out of the Great Hall, leaving Samantha and Lizzie to enjoy the festivities.

Less than five minutes later, with food flying past her antennae and green *antwine* sloshing on her overalls, Samantha stood up and told Lizzie that she'd seen enough of the Silly Season. She wanted to return to their lodgings. Lizzie agreed.

Their two guards met them at the entrance and escorted them away. As they went, the drunken revelry and tuneless jazz songs followed them almost every step of the way to their room (all nine hundred and sixty four of them, according to Lizzie).

Neither wished to see such a sight again.

WHEN LIZZIE STIRRED the next morning, Samantha was already up and dressed in a clean pair of overalls, pacing the floor.

"What's the matter?" Lizzie asked, rubbing her eyes. "I've never seen you so worried."

Samantha stopped pacing. Through the door she could hear the muffled chants of more sewing songs. They had continued without pause through the whole night and even woke her up on one occasion.

"Why don't you tell me what's the matter?" she said. "Our door is still locked and the guards are still outside. We're being kept in here against our will. I know you know something. Don't tell me you don't."

Lizzie eyed one of her bandaged legs and began fiddling with a loose strand of cotton. "You're right. I should have told you from the start," she said. "They brought us here because we don't have the right documentation for passing through their territory. They think we're working for the enemy."

Samantha just stared at her, taking a moment to absorb what she'd heard.

"I told them we were only travelers on our way to Beebylon and didn't know that documentation was required," Lizzie continued. "I also told them that we didn't even know who the enemy was, but they didn't believe me. They said that Beebylon was a fable. It didn't exist."

Samantha paced around some more. "Are you saying that we're prisoners of war?"

"Not exactly. The ants are at war, but it isn't what you think."

Just then the lock turned and an ant entered carrying a clipboard. A pencil was slotted behind her antenna, and at first glance Samantha thought it was the doctor. "Why are you detaining us like prisoners?" Samantha asked.

The ant held up her claw in a gesture of silence and sprayed a perfume that smelled of ginger. She didn't bother to rub antennae with Lizzie or Samantha. "I am not Dr. 1754325Z," she said abruptly. "My name is Sector Manager 8473991B. We look identical because we share the same genes. We're both from the same Clone Mother."

Samantha cocked her antennae. Clones? Now she understood why it was so difficult to tell them apart, and why they spoke with the same melodic tone of voice.

"All the ants in the nest are clones of either the Clone Father or the Clone Mother," Sector Manager 8473991B continued. "We are all genetically perfect and identical. Our fabulous leader, the magnificent Procruste Ant, invented the cloning technique after receiving a vision in his dream. We praise him for our perfect lives."

"What happened to Dr. 1754325Z? Why is she not attending us?" Samantha asked.

"Dr. 1754325Z has been reassigned," the sector manager said with a noncommittal smirk. "I am now responsible for your integration." Then she faced the door and said, "Bring it in!"

Two ants dragged in a large hemp sack and dumped it at the foot of the mysterious wooden machine. Sector Manager 8473991B looked at her watch. "It is now 0900 hours precisely," she said, removing the pencil from behind her antenna and recording the time on the clipboard. "You have until 0900 hours tomorrow to complete your task. We will then assess your entitlement for further privileges."

"Just wait one minute," Samantha said. "You've got no right to hold us prisoners. We're not involved in your war."

Sector Manager 8473991B held up her claw for silence, and sprayed some more ginger perfume. "I suggest you hold your tongue, Miss Honeycomb. Time is ticking, and time is honey."

With that, she left.

IT WAS A while before Lizzie stopped crying and Samantha could get a sentence out of her without a flood of tears. "I'm so sorry," Lizzie said, wiping her eyes with the back of her claw. "It's all my fault. I should never have come with you on this journey."

"That's just plain nonsense, Lizzie McCoon," Samantha said. She sat on the bed and put her arms around Lizzie's shoulder. "You've been ever so brave."

"I just feel so bad."

Lizzie's comment reminded Samantha of something Gerald The Great had said. It seemed such a long time ago, but in fact was only days. "Kite gliding!" she said, and pointed to the whitewashed ceiling.

Lizzie followed her gaze, then turned back to Samantha. "What are you talking about?"

"Oh, nothing," she said, "just something I learned on my travels. Anyway, you mustn't blame yourself for what's happened. Things happen for a reason."

Lizzie sniffled twice and said, "I wish I had your faith. Then things would be so much easier."

Samantha wasn't so sure. Lizzie had forgotten she'd spent a year in prison and was exiled to the Crazy Lands for her beliefs. Just because she had faith didn't mean that her life was easier. In fact, the stronger her faith had become, the more she'd had to endure. She told Lizzie as such. "Take our situation now, for instance," she said.

"What about it? We're prisoners of war," Lizzie said, scratching an arm. "We're going to be here until we die of old age or get executed as spies." She burst into tears again.

The very same thought had passed through Samantha's mind not so long ago. She was reminded of an old parable. A wise master and her disciple were sitting on a water lily in the middle of a pond discussing the nature of life and the mysteries of the Great Mother. Suddenly, out of nowhere, a wild storm blew across the pond. It was too dangerous for them to buzz away, so they decided to ride it out clinging to the lily. The disciple began to fret as the waves became bigger and bigger.

She then yelled out, "Why has the Great Mother made me suffer this storm? Why has she done this to me?" The disciple then let go of the lily to buzz away, but was swept into the pond by a large wave, where she drowned.

The wise master, on the other hand, never once asked why she was made to suffer. All she did was pray that the Great Mother help her through the troubles. Soon after, the storm abated and the wise master buzzed back to the hive. Along the way, she saw the bodies of hundreds of wasps floating in the pond. If it hadn't been for the storm, she and the hive would have been attacked and many would have died. Without asking, she'd learnt the reason why.

Lizzie sniffled again, then said, "What do we do in the meantime?"

Samantha glanced around the room. "Why don't we see what's inside the sack?"

She loosened the thread tying the sack's upper ends. Immediately, white fluffy stuff spilled onto the floor. "Cotton," Lizzie said, picking it up and teasing the fibers.

"Are you sure?" Samantha asked.

"Of course. I'm a caterpillar. Trust me." She gave Samantha a coy wink. "And I'm pretty sure I know what we're supposed to do with it, too."

Lizzie sat down on the strange machine's inbuilt stool. "This is called a spinning wheel," she said. "My family runs a silk factory in the Old Country, where I'm from. Have you heard of McCoon Silk Industries? That's ours. Anyway, we have hundreds of these machines to spin silk for export all around the world. I'm sure spinning cotton is very similar."

Samantha said, "Really, Lizzie, you are full of surprises. How do we do it? I've never seen such a bizarre contraption."

Lizzie gave Samantha a crash course in the use of a spinning wheel. There were lots of parts and names she had to remember, things like flywheel, footman, drive band, spindle, and pedal (which Lizzie called a *treadle*). There was more. "This U-shaped piece of wood is called the flyer," Lizzie said, and pointed to it. "The flyer has hooks to store the yarn evenly on the bobbin when we spin it. It's what gives the twist to the fiber. I'll give you a demonstration of how the whole thing works."

Lizzie grabbed the cord that had tied the sack together. "We'll need this for our leader thread," she said, and tied one end to the centre of the bobbin. "You'll see in a minute what it's for."

She threaded the rest of the leader through the hooks on one side of the flyer, then stuck the free end through an opening in the spindle she called the orifice. "I prefer to tie a loop on the end of my leader so that the fiber holds firm," she said, gently teasing some cotton and threading it into the loop. Then she looked up at Samantha. "Now we're ready to start spinning."

Samantha watched Lizzie depress the treadle. The footman plunged and the flywheel turned. The whole contraption was soon a blur of spinning parts, the whirring flyer pulling the cotton into the orifice, twisting its fibers and spooling the yarn onto the bobbin. After a minute or two, Lizzie stopped pedalling (or *treadling*, as she called it) and inspected the result. The machine slowed to a halt.

"That's amazing," Samantha said. "So this is how they make thread for sewing."

"One way," Lizzie said. "Would you like to give it a go?"

Samantha traded places with Lizzie and began spinning the cotton. It wasn't as easy as it first appeared. Sometimes the cotton broke because she was treadling too fast, which then had to be mended. Sometimes the yarn slipped on the bobbin and the wheel brake had to be tightened.

"Soon you'll be a master," Lizzie said. "We'll have this whole sack spun before dinner time."

Throughout the day they took shifts at sitting at the wheel, and although Lizzie's prediction was a slight underestimation of the time required to finish the work, the last of the cotton spun onto the bobbin around midnight. Samantha collapsed onto her bed, exhausted but a little proud of their achievement, and slept a dreamless sleep.

SECTOR MANAGER 8473991B was full of praise the next morning. Smiling widely, she eyed the spun cotton and the empty hemp sack. "This is simply wonderful," she said, recording data onto her clipboard and spraying a fabulous perfume of concentrated vanilla from her belt. Samantha was excited just smelling it, kind of how lavender made her feel, almost kind of drunk.

"You have an efficiency rating of 0.98," said the sector manager. "This is simply incredible. I have never seen such feat. Wait until our eminent leader hears of this. Your privilege entitlements will surely increase."

"Does that mean we can go for a walk outside?" Samantha asked, hoping to catch the sector manager in a generous mood. She was also thinking of escape. "Bees and caterpillars need sunshine to keep working."

Sector Manager 8473991B scratched the top of her head with the pencil. "I'm not sure if that can be arranged," she said. "You need to have at least one hundred efficiency points before you can mingle with the other POWs outside. But I'll see what I can do. In the meantime, I want you to spin some more cotton."

This time, not one, but two sacks were heaved into the room. Despondent, Samantha just stared at them.

"Come now," the sector manager said, spraying a perfume that smelled of sweetened coconut, "don't look so glum. You have both been so efficient it's only logical to increase your workload. The war effort depends on it." Then she went to the door. "I'll be back at precisely 0900 hours tomorrow. Now, chop, chop! Get to work. Time is ticking, and time is honey."

For all that day and all that night, Samantha and Lizzie worked, stopping only to change shifts. They ate on the job, and improved their efficiency rating from the previous day. While one sat at the wheel and treadled, the other teased and readied the cotton, fixing any snags and urging the other on when she tired. By the time they could hear the changing of the morning guard outside their door at six o'clock, the last of the cotton was spun. They barely had three hours sleep before they were woken.

"This is just un-be-*lievable*," the sector manager said, scribbling on the clipboard. "Simply un-be-lievable. Together you have an efficiency rating of 3.04, which equates to 1.52 each." Spraying some vanilla perfume, she looked up at Samantha and Lizzie, who were barely able to keep their eyes open. "That means you're able to perform one and a half times the work of our most efficient ant. You've set a new benchmark, something to be proud of."

"Does that mean we can have a day off?" asked Samantha, her voice as weary as her eyes.

Sector Manager 8473991B was again scribbling on the clipboard. "What? Yes, of course. Today is Cloneday, the day of rest. On the old calendar it used to be called Sunday. Enjoy it while you can."

They spent the day sleeping. Then the work was piled on the floor again. That week, they spun yards and yards of cotton thread, working long into the nights and waking early before the worms every day – Workday, Sewday, Spinday, Songday, Ant-day, Procrusteday – until finally Cloneday arrived once again and Samantha could rest her weary body and Lizzie could take the weight off her many feet. The sector manager informed them that their efficiency rating had improved even more and that she had received a promotion, to a 3-star Sector Manager. She proudly displayed the new stars sewn to the strap of her overalls and told them she was hoping to make it to 5-star rating within four years. Then she would be eligible for a regional managership, maybe even an entire anthill, who could tell, the world was at her feet. She presented Samantha and Lizzie with a reward for setting a new efficiency record.

"Honeydew," the sector manager said, handing a bowl of little green candy to Samantha. "Go on, try one. The aphids in the lower basement make them." She shook her head, her mind somewhere else. "Irritating things, those aphids. Always getting the unions involved and going on strike. Not very efficient at all." Then she looked up, smiling. "Make damn good honeydew, though. It's not quite the real thing, it isn't honey, but it's an adequate substitute, especially in times of war." Samantha tasted one and agreed it wasn't too bad at all. Lizzie politely declined. "I bet you didn't know that *antwine* is made from fermented honeydew, either," said the sector manager, and paused, as if remembering something important. "Oh, I nearly forgot the main thing."

Samantha and Lizzie shared inquisitive glances as six ants carried in a large cardboard box and set about removing its contents. "What do you think of your new spinning wheel?" she asked.

Samantha and Lizzie eyed the recent addition to the room. It was identical to the old wheel in every detail. Samantha said nothing. Lizzie just scratched the side of her face.

"With two machines your efficiency rating will get even better," Sector Manager 8473991B said. She looked very pleased with herself, like someone who had just done them a big favor. "Consequently, I have ordered three sacks of cotton to be delivered. They should be arriving shortly."

Samantha felt her heart sink into her belly. Her antennae sagged and her wings flopped to her sides. Not even the bowl of honeydew candy could cheer her up.

The sector manager then left, claiming she was late for a very important meeting. She was expecting to receive a framed certificate for Manager of the Month.

The three sacks of cotton were duly delivered and Samantha and Lizzie set to work. Samantha took the new machine, Lizzie the old, and by two o'clock the next morning they were finally able to slip between the stiff, starched sheets and rest their heads on the hard pillows. Every muscle in Samantha's body ached, but she was soon asleep and dreaming of a magical hive where honey dripped from the walls and nobody got sick.

LIKE HER TIME in prison, the weeks passed like an ageing snail. Samantha knew escape wasn't going to be possible until her wings had healed, so she kept spinning cotton and dreaming up escape plans. When the doctors finally did remove the plaster, Samantha was disappointed to see that her wings had withered and stiffened due to inactivity. She told herself that it was just a minor setback, and resolved to make them even stronger than they'd been before they were broken. She adhered to a strict regime of flapping exercises before and after she had finished her work. She even started doing push-ups and sit-ups and lots of other 'up' things that drove Lizzie crazy.

"Do you *have* to do that?" Lizzie asked one morning, lifting her head off her pillow. Her eyes were heavy and full of sleep.

Samantha was buzzing up and down on the spot, up to the ceiling and back to the floor, up and down, up and down, over and over again. Lizzie watched in disgust, then pulled the pillow over her head and went back to sleep. Samantha didn't stop. She was determined to be ready for any opportunity to escape.

As the days passed, Lizzie began to complain of a peculiar itch all over her body. The ant doctors simply put it down to nerves and told her not to worry so much. It wasn't the first time that she'd had it, she told them, but they just reiterated what they'd said. Her appetite too, had increased, as had, Samantha noticed, her waistline. The bowl of honeydew candy now had a permanent place next to Lizzie's spinning wheel and required constant refilling. Samantha wondered why she'd given up on her diet, but didn't ask.

"What do they want with all this thread?" Lizzie said one day while seated at her machine. She was sucking on candy from the bowl and scratching her arm.

"Beats me," Samantha said, also seated at her machine. She was doing some low-impact wing exercises while she worked. "They must need it for the war. Perhaps they use it to make more overalls or trade it for honey." She eyed the boxes stacked against the wall. There were dozens of them, each containing twenty spools of thread. She returned to her work and low-impact wing exercises. She had other things to worry about, like escape.

On the seventh Antday of their capture, Sector Manager 8473991B arrived with an order from the

Venerable Leader, the magnificent Procruste Ant. Samantha and Lizzie's efficiency rating had soared to 2.1 and news of their incredible feats had spun its way to the very top.

"In recognition of the contribution to the war effort," the sector manager said, reading from an official scroll, "it is hereby granted, by decree of His Excellency, the Most Splendid Procruste Ant, to Miss Samantha B. Honeycomb and Miss Lizzie McCoon, the rank of Special Citizen Second Class, effective immediately on this the 53rd day in the year of our Leader, 49."

Samantha desperately hoped that this signified something good, like an end to their imprisonment. She gave Lizzie, who was looking ever so impressed with their new title, an optimistic smile.

Sector Manager 8473991B began rolling up the scroll. She explained that Special Citizen Second Class was the highest possible rank allowable in the constitution for any non-ant. It entitled them to certain privileges, like one half day off every month for educational purposes, a choice of three herbal teas with their meals, and a thirty-minute recreation break on the surface every day.

"So we're not actually free to leave then," said Samantha. "We're just prisoners with a fancy title."

The 3-star sector manager seemed irritated. "I know a lot of POWs who would kill to have that title and the advantages that come with it. If you want, I can relay the message to the fabulous Procruste Ant that you reject his honorable gift."

Samantha lowered her head in disappointment. "No, don't do that. Tell him we accept the honor with gratitude and bid him thanks."

"That's better. I'll arrange for the guards to escort you to the surface for your rec-break at 1700 hours.

Till then, keep spinning. Time is ticking, and time is honey."

Samantha waited for the door to close and the lock to turn before she spoke. "Reet Bee-teet! This might be our chance to escape," she said to Lizzie, who had already taken her seat at the spinning wheel. "When the guards take us to the surface, we'll make a break for it. If we get separated, we'll rendezvous at the giant teapot where we met, okay?"

Lizzie stopped treadling and the flywheel slowly came to a halt. "Are you sure that's such a wise thing, Samantha? What if they recapture us? We'll lose all the privileges and entitlements we've worked so hard for. They'll even rescind our status as Special Citizens Second Class."

Samantha crossed her antennae and stared at Lizzie in disbelief. "Are you saying you don't even want to take the chance?"

"All I'm saying is that I don't want to risk everything we've gained."

"And what about gaining back what was taken from us, our freedom?"

Lizzie began treadling the wheel, silently fuming with anger. Then she stopped. "Do you really want to risk everything for freedom, even your life?" she asked. "Because I'm not sure I do."

Now Samantha felt angry. Her face flushed, her heart thumped, and her wings flapped erratically. "Do you call this a life?" she said, spreading her arms. What little floor space was not filled with boxes of spun and un-spun cotton was occupied by the large spinning wheels. "There's barely enough space to breathe in here. It makes me claustrophobic."

"Then we'll just have to ask Sector Manager 8473991B for a bigger room." Lizzie's machine was now in full flight again. "I'm sure she'd arrange it if she thought our efficiency rating would improve. It wouldn't be difficult."

Samantha couldn't believe what she was hearing. "I'm beginning to think you actually like it here," she said.

Lizzie glanced up from the spinning wheel. "Is it really so bad? We have a roof over our head, we get three full meals a day, now with a choice of three herbal teas, and we're valued citizens, albeit second-class. Everybody raves about how efficient we are and what a good contribution we're making to the war effort. We have purpose here. You're always saying everything happens for a reason. Well, maybe we've found our reason." She went back to work.

Samantha crossed her antennae again, glaring at Lizzie, thinking what to say, or more to the point, what not to say. "We *are* here for a reason," she said, "but this is only one step along the road to our ultimate destination, that is all."

"Have you thought that this might be *my* Bee Dream?" Lizzie said, not looking up. She began scratching furiously at an itch on one of her legs. "All things considered, I could have a very comfortable life here."

Samantha sat down at her wheel and began spinning, her jaw clenched, thinking that only a blind bee would choose a flowerpot in preference to a meadow.

For the rest of the day they said not a word to each other. The only sound in the room was the whir of the spinning wheels and the chants of ants singing praises of sewing somewhere down the corridor.

At PRECISELY 1700 hours, two guards entered the room. At spear point, Samantha and Lizzie were escorted through the twisting maze of whitewashed corridors, up and up and up, until finally they reached the uppermost level of the anthill. Lizzie whispered to Samantha that they had just climbed fourteen floors; their room was deep underground.

At the bottom of the last flight of stairs, Samantha looked directly above. The opening to the upper surface was an exposed ring of daylight, like the mouth of a cave, beckoning her to the outside world and freedom.

"I know what you're thinking," one of the guards said, "and as a precaution we have a little deterrent for you."

The guards then tied the base of her wings together with thick cotton rope. Several of Lizzie's legs were also tied, making it difficult to walk and impossible to run. They weren't going to get very far with these, Samantha mused. She would just have to be patient and assess the situation as it came.

With one guard leading, and one behind, Samantha and Lizzie climbed the steps into the open air. Samantha closed her eyes atop the anthill and inhaled deeply. After the sterility of the corridors, the fresh air was divine. Before the guards marched them down the western face, she quickly surveyed the scene, hoping to establish a future route of escape. She was totally unprepared for what she saw.

All this time spent captive inside the anthill, she had assumed she was still somewhere in the field of golden sunflowers. She was mistaken. There were no sunflowers within sight. Indeed, there were no flowers of any kind. Large, forbidding pine trees blocked out all but a few scattered rays of the sun, casting cool, dark shadows upon the forest floor. Dozens of anthills the color of dark caramel, or burnt honey, dominated the immediate landscape, like a range of miniature volcanoes. Beyond them meandered a steady moving stream. She scanned the western horizon, hopeful of catching a glimpse of the forested hills and the lake. There was nothing other than the sun topping the pine trees. She felt such a surge of despair that tears began falling down her cheeks. Even if she managed to escape one day, there was nowhere for her to go. She was completely and utterly lost.

"Isn't it wonderful to be in the open air?" she heard Lizzie say. "Sometimes you don't know what you have until its gone."

"Like freedom," Samantha mumbled.

The rear guard prodded her in the back with his spear and she began descending the face of the anthill. She saw endless columns of ants marching along well-worn tracks to and from the anthills, many laden with assorted items – pieces of wood, scraps of metal, strips of material – and as they disappeared into the anthills, more ants emerged to trek off into the woods and gather whatever booty they could find.

"It must be for the war effort," Lizzie said, following Samantha's gaze.

At the bottom of the anthill, the guards ordered them to head for the stream. It was actually more like a river, and Samantha's heart lifted; it probably flowed into the lake. As they approached the clear waters, her mind was so full with ideas of escape she wasn't paying attention to where she was walking. Lizzie's abrupt warning to "Look out!" jerked her back.

She lowered her eyes and saw a gaping hole. One more step and she would have fallen straight into it. "That was close," she said with her claw over her racing heart.

The guards laughed and prodded them with their spears. "That's the work of Mad Jack Hammer," one said. "Next time you'd better watch your step!"

Mad Jack Hammer, it seemed, had dug dozens and dozens of holes in and around the riverbank, but he was nowhere to be seen. Samantha and Lizzie plotted a course through the minefield and eventually made it to water's edge. Downstream, about halfway to the first bend, a chain gang of red ants in blue- and white-striped overalls were filling sandbags with the dirt Mad Jack had excavated. Other ants then piled the sandbags against eroded sections of the riverbank.

Oblivious to them, a white figure was swimming in the river. Pointing to the unknown bug, Samantha asked the guards who it was.

"That's Mad Jack," the rear guard said, snorting. "He swims and digs holes for himself. That's all he does, every day."

Samantha and Lizzie watched Mad Jack swim against the current. He swam and swam and swam, getting nowhere. After a while, he seemed to tire. The current was clawing him backward, but he still kept trying. Then, seemingly defeated, he swam to the shore and waded wearily onto the bank.

"He's a termite," Samantha said.

"How grotesque," Lizzie said, with a shudder.

Mad Jack headed to a pile of clothes at the base of an upright spade, dried himself off, then picked up a pair of dirt-stained overalls and slipped them on. Grabbing his spade in one motion, he started to dig. Dirt flew over his shoulder at a rapid rate. The guards laughed and taunted him to dig faster. Before long he was standing knee-deep in a hole.

Samantha wandered over and offered him some honeydew candy she was keeping in her overall pocket. "What are you digging for?" she asked.

Mad Jack took the candy, but didn't say a word. He wiped the sweat off his brow and kept digging. Dirt flew over his shoulder, piling around the rim of the hole, dirt the chain gang would later use to reinforce the riverbank. After who knows how many more minutes of silent digging, Samantha gave up and returned to Lizzie and the guards. The half hour rec-break was almost over.

Later that evening, as she spun the last thread of cotton and got ready for bed, Samantha pondered the strangeness of Mad Jack. She was perplexed at his determination to dig holes for himself and swim against the current. Just who was crazier, though, Mad Jack or the ants?

She glanced at Lizzie, already tucked in bed and asleep, and wondered if this, as she had said, really was her Bee Dream.

LIKE AN ANT song, the days came and went. The journey to the lake was barely mentioned anymore, and for Samantha spinning cotton helped to pass the time. Though outwardly satisfied with three good meals and a choice of herbal teas every day, there was a void as deep as one of Mad Jack's holes in her life. Sure, she had the security of a roof over her head and a job that offered promotion. Sure, she had the acceptance of her peers (wasn't she a Special Citizen Second Class?); but there was something missing, and its very absence was getting her down – joy.

Lizzie, though, wasn't as put out with her new life. "I have to admit," she said one evening before rec-break, scratching an itch on her face, "it's far more than I ever expected. My father always said I never had a purpose in my life."

Lizzie's remarks were beginning to annoy Samantha, more so when she waved off the injustice of their captivity with a tired, mechanical reply, "Really, Samantha, you think that freedom's the only thing worth living for." Or when she said, "Who really is free, anyway? The honeybees and the caterpillars starving to death in the outside world, or us, who at least have food in our bellies and a bed to sleep in?"

It was pointless arguing. Unlike Lizzie, she would never be happy with these whitewashed walls and bags of cotton. Her destiny was elsewhere.

Early one morning (although living underground had distorted her sense of time, she thought it might be the month of August, or Honeymoon, as the ants called it), Samantha was woken with a start. Lizzie was sitting on the end of her bed, rocking back and forth and muttering something about it happening again. She didn't seem to notice Samantha. Her antennae were rigid and she was hugging her chest, almost crushing herself.

Samantha had also spotted something else. Something that was lying on the ground between the beds that wasn't there last night. It was thin and wrinkly, like a crumpled sheet, and long and hollow, at least as long as Lizzie. She had seen something similar when she met Lizzie at the giant teapot.

"What's the matter?" she asked.

"It's happened again," Lizzie moaned, hugging her chest and rocking back and forth as she had. "I've molted! Do you know what that means?"

Samantha shook her head. Bees didn't molt.

Lizzie threw her head back and moaned, long and loud, drowning out the background sewing chants. "I'm going to shed my skin three more times and then I'm going to go through metamorphosis." Lizzie now began to sob uncontrollably. "I'm scared, Samantha," she said. "I'm afraid something terrible will happen when I pupate. I don't want to die."

Samantha sat next to Lizzie and gave her a hug, telling her not to worry, that it wasn't so bad, that the change was a necessary part of a caterpillar's life. Besides, if something went wrong, which it surely wouldn't, as Special Citizens Second Class they were entitled to the best healthcare honey could buy. Metamorphosis was nothing to worry about. It was a doddle. She could say that because she'd been through it herself.

Lizzie shook her head, sniveling a bit. "I'm still frightened, Samantha," she said, staring blankly at the wrinkled skin at her feet. "I know all caterpillars have to go through it, but that still doesn't mean I want to do it. I like being a caterpillar. I like being me. Why do I have to change?"

Samantha recalled the fears she herself had had when she pupated. She knew this was something Lizzie had to conquer herself. "I want you to know that when your time comes to pupate, no matter what happens, I'll be there to help and support you through it."

Her words seemed to be of some comfort. Lizzie stopped rocking and moaning, at least.

The background chanting didn't, however, abate one bit.

LATER THAT WEEK they were transferred to a much larger room, one of the minor halls requisitioned from an overall factory that had fallen well below sustainable efficiency quotas. The sector manager who'd been in charge was sent for reconditioning, and was later seen filling sandbags with the red ants at the riverbank.

"How do you like your new accommodations?" Sector Manager 8473991B asked, ushering them into the now empty chamber. She sprayed a tangy perfume with peppermint and lemon and a touch of basil.

"It's fantastic," Lizzie said. She began to point and speak fast. "We can store the un-spun cotton in that corner. We can put the spinning wheels in the middle over here. And we can store the spun cotton near the door, where it can be collected. We can do so much to this place. Our efficiency rating is going to improve even more. I just know it."

The sector manager smiled knowingly. "I want to show you something," she said, "something very few non-ants have ever seen. I hope it will inspire you to greater and greater feats."

Samantha and Lizzie followed her to a part of the anthill they had never been. As they meandered down the corridor, the chanting became noticeably louder.

This is my needle!
This is my thread!
This is the work that earns our bread!
Left, right, left, right.

Sector Manager 8473991B stopped outside a guarded door. Atop was a sign: THROUGH SEWING COMES FREEDOM. "It's in here," she said, raising her voice over the chanting.

One for the sunshine!
One for the snow!
This is the way we patch and sew!
Left, right, left, right.

She mumbled a password to the guards and they opened the doors. The noise roared out:

We are the ants that mend your pants!
Left, right, left, right.
We never say never
And we never say can't!

Left, right, left, right!
Whether we sleep,
Or whether we fight,
We sew all day and we sew all night!

In a chamber larger than the Procruste Ant Inc. Great Hall, rows upon rows upon rows of ants sat sewing, needle and thread in one claw, sewing item in the other. Between the rows were high mounds of finished articles: antennae warmers, overalls, and other items of apparel. In regimented fashion, the ants sewed to the rhythm of their chants. In went the needle. Out went the needle. In went the needle again. Not one ant missed a beat.

"This is just one of our sewing factories. There are literally hundreds throughout the anthill," Sector Manager 8473991B shouted. "All of them are using the cotton thread you've spun. As you can see, the war effort's progressing marvelously."

"Why do you need so many clothes?" Samantha asked, also shouting. "Wouldn't spears and shields and armor be more useful?"

"Oh, no, no, no," the sector manager shouted, shaking her head. "The arms market is dead. It's clothing we need. We're fighting a rag trade war, not a territorial one." She then gestured toward the factory floor and smiled proudly. The ants kept sewing and chanting. "Our splendiferous Leader taught us that we must fight our battles on the economic front. We must sacrifice everything in our pursuit of honey. Profits are the only way to appease the God of Science."

The sector manager then ushered Samantha and Lizzie back to their new quarters. "I want you to think about what you saw today," she said before leaving, "because I have a proposal for you. I want you to consider setting up a spinning factory. You'll both be sub-managers in your own right, although only second-class, but it'll be worth your while, believe me."

Lizzie was visibly excited. They could use McCoon Silk Industries as a model, she told Samantha later. "Just think of it. Our efficiency rating will be out of this world. We'll double the war effort single-handedly. The profits will be huge."

Samantha agreed to at least give it a try, keeping her reasons to herself. It would be a great cover for the escape plan she had begun to formulate.

I<small>T</small> <small>WASN'T</small> <small>LONG</small> before the first spinning factory known to the ants was established: Procruste Ant Cotton Inc. Samantha and Lizzie were given honorary sub-managerial positions and separate sleeping quarters. In addition, a personal security guard was assigned to each of them, though Samantha disliked Lieutenant 7725695P immediately. Although he allowed her a certain degree of privacy, she was always aware of his presence, whether he was waiting just outside her door, or whether he was watching her in the factory, silent and broody. The measure was for her own safety, or so Sector Manager 8473991B said, but Samantha had suspicions that the lieutenant was passing on information of her every move to those in positions of power, even to the very top.

So to keep a low profile, she busied herself with the redevelopment of the factory, which proceeded at a rapid pace. "It's not that much smaller than my father's silk factory," Lizzie said one morning. She had now taken on the habit of carrying a clipboard and slotting a pencil behind her antenna. She also wore a belt laden with personally engraved perfume bottles. "Though with the modifications we've drawn up, it should be exceedingly more efficient."

After the safety checks had been completed, the next phase of construction involved the installment of the machinery. Working around the clock, factory ants assembled ninety-seven spinning wheels in less than six days. As they did, Samantha trained the first fifteen ants in the art of spinning cotton. They were to become trainers and 1-star floor managers in the ensuing weeks.

"I've been looking at the factory in relation to its position in the anthill," Samantha said to Lizzie on the floor during one lunch break, "and I think that if we tunneled another corridor directly to the main sewing factory, we'd cut at least fifteen minutes off transportation time."

Lizzie sprayed some vanilla scent into the air and scribbled something down on the clipboard. "Fifteen minutes?" she said, putting the pencil to her mouth and doing some mental arithmetic. "That'll improve our efficiency by… by… by at least 12.5%. Reet Bee-teet!"

She told Samantha to wait for a minute and then dashed to her office, returning with a scrolled map of the anthill left behind by the previous sector manager. She unrolled the map and held it up. "Yes …yes, I see it now. Brilliant. Just brilliant," she said, and lowered the map to look at Samantha. "You know, I always knew you'd come around some day. We belong here, you and me." She scrolled up the map and sprayed some peppermint perfume. "I'll let Sector Manager 8473991B know that you'll be taking charge of the new tunnel."

Samantha watched Lizzie head back to her office with relief. The first part of her escape plan had gone relatively smoothly. The second part, getting Mad Jack to dig a secret tunnel from the surface to meet the new transportation tunnel, would be a lot more difficult.

UP ON THE surface for the next seven evenings, Samantha tried to make conversation with Mad Jack. She figured her first priority was to find out what motivated him to dig so many holes. She brought him honeydew candy to break the ice, which he devoured but still wouldn't talk. He just kept digging and digging. The guards laughed at her attempts, including Lizzie and her personal security guard. Lieutenant 7725695P, however, didn't even crack a smile. He just watched from a distance, staring and taking note of everything she did.

Below the surface in the meantime, sixteen days ahead of schedule, the spinning factory was officially opened. Samantha and Lizzie received a Manager of the Month Award and promotion to the rank of 2-star sub-sector manager. Within four weeks, Procruste Ant Cotton Inc. had become the most profitable and efficiently run company within the anthill. The new transportation tunnel was well underway and everything was running smoothly. Moreover, Lizzie was proving to be more than just a handy spinner of cotton. She was also an extremely capable accounts manager, an absolute whiz with numbers.

"It must have been all the practice counting my steps," she said to Samantha at the end of the first operating month. They were lunching in her office, scrutinizing the latest efficiency figures. "Numbers just seem to come naturally to me."

In the background, the chants of the ants on the factory floor almost drowned out her words:

> *We don't moan,*
>> *And we don't cry,*
> *'Coz spin-ning cott'n makes us fly!*
> *One, two, three, four.*

We make thread that's thick or thin!
One, two, three, four.
'Coz we're ants
Who love to spin!

At the end of the following month, Lizzie was privy to a rumor (though she wouldn't say who had let her in on the secret) that they were going to receive a special pardon from the splendiferous Procruste Ant, as part of his upcoming birthday celebrations. Apparently, he was going to issue a decree entitling them to acquire property in sector VB-52, a very exclusive area on the east side of the anthill. They were moving up in the world, as Lizzie had become fond of saying.

Samantha, herself, only wanted to escape this maddening anthill of job promotions and property accumulation; but by the time the new transportation tunnel was complete, she still had yet to get one word out of Mad Jack Hammer. All he did was dig and dig. Every evening she brought him honeydew candy. Every evening he ate it without a word, and every evening she was escorted back to her lodgings more and more frustrated. She felt as if everything in the world was conspiring to keep her from reaching her Bee Dream.

She was sitting on the edge of one of Mad Jack's deep pits one evening at rec-break, watching him dig, and not in a particularly good mood. Mad Jack was typically silent. Dirt flew from his spade and landed outside the hole. She had tried everything she possibly could to speak to him and was on the verge of giving up all together. Nothing had changed in the past two months, apart from a lot more holes in the riverbank.

"You know," she sighed, "we're not so dissimilar, you and I. We're both searching for something and getting nowhere. I've been trying to find Beebylon, and you're trying to find... well, I don't know what you're trying to find."

All of a sudden, Mad Jack stopped digging and looked up. His brow was smudged with dirt, as were his cheeks and arms and overalls. "Did you say Beebylon?" he asked.

Samantha was so startled she almost fell into the pit. She stared down at him, then glanced over her wings at the security guards. They were with Lizzie further upstream, watching the chain gang reinforce the riverbank, which was becoming more and more eroded each time she came to the surface. They had got bored of watching her trying to talk to Mad Jack a long time ago. Even the unsmiling Lieutenant 7725695P seemed no longer interested in what she was doing.

She looked down at Mad Jack again. "You... you can talk," she said.

"Of course I can talk," he said, leaning on his spade. "I'm a termite. Tell me what you know of Beebylon."

There was very little time left before rec-break was over. Samantha quickly whispered what little she'd heard, that Beebylon was a magical hive built high upon a cliff where everyone was rich and no-body got sick.

"And where honey drips from the walls," Mad Jack added, staring up at the sky with dreamy eyes. Then he sighed, preparing to dig again. "But it's just a fable. It doesn't exist."

"What if I told you where it is?" she said. Mad Jack looked back up, the spade sticking into the bottom of the pit. "It's at the lake."

"I know of no lake," Mad Jack said, stretching as high as he could to peer over the rim of the pit. "There's only this river, and it has no end."

At that moment, Samantha heard footsteps approaching from behind. Rec-break was over. Mad Jack hurried back to digging and Samantha was taken to her lodgings, all the while trying to hide her smile from the guards.

As the days went by, little by little, Samantha began to earn the trust of Mad Jack. Unbeknown to the guards and Lizzie, they discussed many things, the ants, the war effort, Samantha's capture and detainment, but most of all, Beebylon. After a week, Samantha tentatively mentioned the possibility of escape. Mad Jack wasn't interested in the slightest. He had an important mission to achieve. He was searching for something.

"Just what do you hope to find digging all these holes?" Samantha asked in frustration. He had just started on a new pit close to the water's edge.

"Honeyroot," Mad Jack said.

Honeyroot? The magical root that turned stone into honey, the secret to Infinite Richness? Samantha couldn't believe it. Queen Beetrix had sent her into the Crazy Lands to bring back that very same thing; without it the High Priestess would continue to usurp her power. Without it Samantha would never see her parents again. She flapped her wings excitedly, despite them being tied together.

"I know where to find it," she whispered. The guards and Lizzie were standing within earshot.

Mad Jack kept on digging, dirt flying over the rim of the pit. "I've heard that before," he said. "I'm not stupid, you know. I've been searching for honeyroot since before you were born. What makes you think you know better?"

"What have you got to lose?" she said, and then walked away, praying he'd taken the bait. She could now concentrate on getting the next phase of the plan into motion.

THE NEXT DAY on the surface, Samantha completely ignored Mad Jack. She spent the time chatting with Lizzie and the security guards, even though she could see him out the corner of her eyes waving his spade and trying to attract her attention.

This she allowed to carry on over the next few days, during which she secretly copied the map of the anthill that Lizzie kept in her filing cabinet. The map was high priority, so that Mad Jack knew exactly where to dig, but extremely risky business. Not the least because she had to sneak into Lizzie's office while she was away from her desk at lunch break or at meetings with other managers or union leaders.

When she went to the surface in the meantime, she continued to ignore Mad Jack. She could tell he was at his wit's end. Sometimes he would act as if he had dropped his spade on his foot and jump around pretending to be in pain. Lizzie and the guards would laugh, not knowing that it was just a ruse for getting Samantha's attention. At other times, he'd amble over to where she was standing with the others and begin to dig a hole right behind her. He would even deliberately toss dirt onto her feet, trying to get her to say something. She never did, but she wasn't going to make him wait for too much longer.

While Lizzie was at a meeting with a health and safety inspector the following week, Samantha snuck into her office to make the final amendments to the map she was copying. She went to the filing cabinet and removed the scrolled map. She could hear the ant chants from the factory floor. Somehow, they seemed louder than usual. On the back wall, next to the framed awards for Special Citizen Second Class and Sub-Manager of the Month, a portrait of Procruste Ant glared down upon her. Uneasy at his stare, she removed the copied map she kept folded in her overall pocket and unrolled the scroll on top of the desk. She was just about to begin copying when Lizzie burst into the office.

"There you are!" Lizzie said, raising her voice. "I've been looking all over for you."

Samantha stared back, not knowing what to do. "I... I thought you were at a meeting," she said.

"Something came up. I cancelled it." Lizzie shut the door, muffling the outside chants. Her gaze then fell to the desk and the splayed scroll. "What are you doing?" she asked, coming over to get a better look.

Samantha could see her whole escape plan disappearing down one of Mad Jack's holes. She was done for. She had to say something – anything – she couldn't hide what she'd done anymore. "I didn't want to tell you this just yet," she began, "but... but I was planning on digging a tunnel to..."

"To connect the transportation tunnel directly with the central corridor," Lizzie finished, her claw tracing an imaginary route on the map she thought the tunnel would take. "It's brilliant, Samantha. It'll cut thirty minutes off our delivery times. Why didn't you tell me about this before?"

It was a moment before Samantha could think clearly. "You were just so busy," she said. "I didn't want to disturb you." She released the breath she hadn't known she was holding. "Anyway, why did you want to see me?"

Lizzie continued to stare at the map. "Oh, it's nothing. I just molted again this morning, that's all." Lizzie glanced up. Her eyes were sad. "I guess I'll just have to accept the inevitable, won't I?"

Despite the mixture of emotions she felt for her friend, Samantha left the office determined to speak to Mad Jack that evening and give him the copy of the map. They had to start digging. The time for waiting was over; she couldn't afford to risk any more near misses. Anyway, it couldn't have turned out much better, really. The building of the new connecting tunnel would divert the ants' attention from any noise Mad Jack might make as he dug into the anthill. It was perfect.

The Great Mother works in mysterious ways, she thought on her way out of the factory.

On the surface at rec-break, she saw Mad Jack digging a hole halfway to the water's edge. Dirt sprayed from his shovel at a rapid pace. While Lizzie strolled with the lieutenants further upstream, Samantha excused herself to stay nearer the anthill. When they had wandered far enough away, she went to speak with Mad Jack.

When her shadow fell upon him he looked up. "Why've you been ignoring me?" he said. "I want to help you escape. I want to go to Beebylon."

"Not so loud," she whispered. She glanced over at Lizzie and the lieutenants. They weren't looking, so she removed the copied map from her overalls.

Mad Jack stared at it, confused for a moment, then said, "It's like a treasure map."

Samantha kind of agreed: her treasure was freedom. She told him to use it as a guide to tunnel from the water's edge into the transportation tunnel. No one would suspect what he's doing because he always dug. When the tunnel was complete, he'd let her know by signaling with his spade. Then, on the night of the next new moon, she would escape and rendezvous with him at the first bend in the river.

Mad Jack nodded, and agreed not to talk to her again until they'd escaped.

OVER THE NEXT few days, despite the calmness of her exterior, Samantha's mind was in a state of minor chaos. She couldn't concentrate on her work. She couldn't sleep. She couldn't eat. It seemed she couldn't do anything other than worry about getting caught.

As a pretence to supervising the work on the new connecting tunnel, she spent a great deal of time in the transportation tunnel alert for any sign of Mad Jack nearing the completion of his diggings; and by the end of the third week, four days before the new moon, she heard a noise above the ceiling, a kind of scraping she hadn't previously heard.

Reet Bee-teet! she thought. Her heart skipped a beat and her wings flapped in erratic, short bursts. She peered up at the spot where she had heard the noise. There was a damp patch, from which droplets slowly formed and then dripped onto the floor.

"I always knew this anthill was built too close to the river," she heard the lieutenant say from behind.

Samantha spun around and saw Lieutenant 772-5695P glancing up at the wet patch. "I... I... I think it must be water seeping from the top," she said, as calmly as she could.

"I think that's highly unlikely," he said, spraying some musky perfume that made Samantha wince. The scent reminded her of her first encounter with the ants, and she now realized what it signified: danger. "It's never happened before," the lieutenant added. "It must be something else."

She had to think of something quickly. "Maybe it's a reservoir of mud."

"That's possible," he said, thoughtfully. "Still, I think we should have our engineers look at it. Better to be safe. We don't want the whole anthill to be flooded."

Samantha agreed to inform the engineers. The tunnel was her responsibility, after all. The lieutenant told her to be quick. There was a storm front passing through this evening and the tunnel should be reinforced as quickly as possible. Samantha promised she'd hop to it and told him not to worry; it was as good as done. "Hurry up then," he said.

Samantha hurried toward the factory, glad to get away from the snooping lieutenant, at least for a minute. Informing the engineers, though, would be the last thing she would do. If they discovered Mad Jack's tunnel, it was as good as over. There was no other choice. She would have to escape tonight.

As a ruse to keep the lieutenant's curiosity at bay, she had several ants prop the wet ceiling with support beams. She wanted it to look as though the engineers were doing something about it. Later, at rec-break, she told Mad Jack about the change of plan.

"I thought we'd agreed not to speak until we rendezvoused," Mad Jack said, popping his head out of the hole in which he was digging. It was a diversionary hole, in the unlikely event a guard wanted to know what he was doing.

"Things have changed. Lieutenant 7725695P is suspicious of the wet patch. We've got less than twenty-four hours before they discover your tunnel."

Mad Jack glanced up at the evening sky. "I don't like it," he said. "Not a bit. Those clouds mean rain. It's too dangerous. The tunnel could collapse. The river could swell. Anything could happen."

"We've got no choice. It has to be tonight."

Mad Jack relented. He told Samantha everything was as ready as it could be. He wished her luck and confirmed their rendezvous point, just past the first bend in the river. Samantha then left to join Lizzie and the security guards at the water's edge.

Lieutenant 7725695P, she saw, was eying her suspiciously.

THAT NIGHT SAMANTHA didn't bother going back to her lodgings. She spent the time on the factory floor tinkering with the spinning wheels. She was going to miss this anthill, even though she was no more than a glorified prisoner. She was going to miss the chanting, the sector manager, the evening rec-breaks, and, dare she even think it, even the Silly Season. Still, she wasn't going to dwell on it. There was a destiny with her name on it she needed to find.

She waited until the absolute last minute before confronting Lizzie. Although it went against her better judgment, she was going to offer Lizzie the chance to escape with her. If she wanted to stay in the anthill, then that was fine. She wasn't going force her to do something she didn't want to do.

Hoping her friend would come to her senses, Samantha summoned her courage and crossed the factory floor to Lizzie's office. Lizzie was going over the monthly accounts behind her desk. "I've got something to tell you," Samantha said, shutting the door.

"I know, Samantha," Lizzie said, without a trace of surprise. "You're planning on escaping tonight. We know about the tunnel."

Samantha was so shocked she stood frozen to the ground, unable to reply.

"Lieutenant 7725695P has been on to you for a while now. He knew you and Mad Jack were getting up to no good. When he saw the water dripping from the roof of the transportation tunnel today, his suspicions were confirmed. He told me everything. As we speak, Mad Jack is being taken to a prison cell. It's over. Your plan has failed."

The office door opened and in walked Lieutenant 7725695P, smiling. He grabbed Samantha's arm and told her that she was under arrest until their splendiferous leader, the magnificent Procruste Ant, decided on her punishment.

Samantha jerked her arm away. "Take your filthy claws off me," she said, more furious at her friend than with the lieutenant. Then to Lizzie: "Why are you doing this? You know this isn't my Bee Dream."

Lizzie's expression momentarily hardened. "You know your problem, Samantha? You fail to see that Bee Dreams are just that, dreams. Heavens above, you still believe in Beebylon."

Samantha was momentarily taken off guard. She suddenly recalled the old actress in her dream. *To bee or not to bee*, she had said. "And you know your problem?" Samantha said, her body tensing. "You're so frightened of becoming a butterfly and living your destiny that you can't stand to see anyone else living theirs. What kind of a caterpillar are you?"

"Enough!" Lizzie said, and thumped the table with a clenched claw. She began spraying musk-scented perfume in the air. She sprayed and sprayed and sprayed, until the whole bottle was empty. "Take her to her room!" she said to the lieutenant. "Now!"

Lieutenant 7725695P grabbed Samantha's arm, but like before she shook him off. He escorted her to her room without a word. Waiting until she had heard the key in the lock, she threw herself onto the bed and buried her face in the pillow to muffle her cries. It did practically nothing to muffle the chanting down the corridor, however.

When she had cried herself out, she pulled the sheets up over her head in despair. Everything she had worked for was in ruin. She wondered what punishment she'd receive, and what would happen to Mad Jack. She felt guilty at that; if it weren't for her, he wouldn't be locked up in some prison cell.

Mercifully, sleep came and smothered her pain in a blanket of darkness.

SAMANTHA WAS REVISITING an old forgotten dream, buzzing through an endless field of crimson roses, when all of a sudden she heard loud raps on the door and shouting outside. It sounded like one of the guards on nightshift.

Still a little groggy, she slipped out of bed and into her overalls. The rapping ceased and keys rattled in the lock. The door flung open.

"Miss Samantha, quick!" the guard said. His feet, to her surprise, were wet. The whole corridor was flooded. "To the surface!"

She felt the hairs prick on the back of her wings. There was a pungent smell of musk in the air. The chanting had fallen eerily silent.

"The storm's hit!" the guard said. "The river has swelled. Water's pouring down the escape tunnel. We don't know which one of Mad Jack's holes to plug." He grabbed her arm and pulled her into the sodden corridor. Why the ants didn't get Mad Jack from the prison cell instead, she didn't know. "Come on! We have to leave. The anthill's flooding."

Samantha was now fully awake. "We have to get Lizzie," she said.

"She's already on her way to the top," the guard said, pulling her after him. "She's with Lieutenant 7725695P."

They came to the busy intersection with the main corridor. The water was deeper there, almost half-way up Samantha's legs. A multitude of black ants sloshed past in maddened panic, wading toward the stairs and spraying musk-scented perfume. Many were carrying larvae on their backs. As she tried to join the mayhem, Samantha was buffeted to and fro in the scramble to exit the anthill. She tripped and fell to the wet floor. The guard helped her to her feet, but when he took her arm, an hysterical ant spraying musk elbowed Samantha in the back, as if he didn't even see her, and she fell, face first, back into the water. She lifted her head to breathe. All she could see was splashing water and a flurry of legs. She heard the guard shout to get up, then felt him jerk her arm and drag her along the corridor.

Eventually, they managed to scramble to the surface with the horde of ants. Atop the anthill, to her surprise, the guard shackled her wings. He apologized as he did. He was only following orders.

Samantha didn't reply, taking the moment to catch her breath and survey the scene. It was just before dawn and the sky was dark and angry. Heavy raindrops splashed to the ground. Lightning flashed in the east, briefly illuminating the surrounding area. Like black lava from erupting volcanoes, an inestimable number of ants streamed out of the adjacent anthills into the nearby forest, taking their young eggs with them. Lightning flashed again. The river, to her horror, was dangerously high and about to burst its banks.

Urged on by the guard, Samantha trudged down the face of the anthill to the river. Although most of the ants had fled into the woods in search of higher ground, a good number, mostly guards, had rushed to the riverbank. Several of them, including Lieutenant 7725695P and Lizzie, were filling sandbags and passing them along a chain to reinforce the bank.

"You have to show us the mouth of the tunnel," Lizzie said as Samantha approached. "Mad Jack jumped into the river before the guards detained him. You're our only hope of saving the anthills. They're all connected. Once one is flooded, they all are."

Samantha pointed to a group of seven holes near the water's edge. One of them was the mouth. Samantha, Lizzie and the guards rushed over to inspect them. The water lipping over the bank made it impossible to tell which was which. They simply had no choice. They would have to plug each one.

Samantha began scooping dirt into the sandbag Lizzie was holding. The lieutenant and the other guards did likewise. Lightning flashed again. It fizzed overhead, striking a nearby pine tree, which burst into flames and toppled into the river. Several of the guards panicked and ran for the woods. One slipped and fell into a deep pit, his screams easily heard over the deluge.

There was no time to help him. Water was still lipping over the top of the riverbank. Although she felt she was fighting a losing battle, Samantha kept scooping dirt into the sandbags for another ten or so minutes. Lightning flashed and thunder roared. Rain pelted down. It was then, as she bent down to scoop up more dirt, Samantha saw Lizzie's legs. They were free.

"I think we might just do it," Lizzie said.

Samantha stopped for a moment to assess the situation. The holes were steadily filling with dirt and the sandbags reinforcing the riverbank were holding back the water. To her surprise, their efforts were actually starting to make some headway. Samantha returned to filling the sandbags, and at that moment saw something truly terrifying.

"Look out!" she yelled, pointing upstream. Where the pine tree had toppled into the river, part of the riverbank had now begun to sink in and give way, triggering a terrible chain of events. As she'd previously suspected, Mad Jack's excavations had weakened the surrounding riverbank. The ground could barely sustain its own weight. It collapsed under the rush of water, creating a chute through which the river poured, sweeping all before it.

In a matter of seconds, the watery avalanche struck Samantha and Lizzie. They didn't even have time to turn and run.

PART THREE

As THE WATER carried Samantha downstream, her first reaction was to try and fly, but her wings were tied. She struggled against the swirling current, going under several times, knowing she didn't have much time. Leaves and logs and branches swept past her. She snatched at a large twig, but an eddy pulled her under and by the time she'd resurfaced, coughing and spluttering and gasping for air, the twig was well out of reach.

Samantha was now desperate. Lizzie was nowhere in sight and the cold water was sapping her energy. She was finding it more and more difficult to keep afloat. Then she went under for the seventh or eighth time. She fought to the surface, but her head bumped into something hard, preventing her from rising any further, as if she were in a flooded tunnel and her head had just hit the ceiling. She kicked her legs and flailed her arms in panic. Her head hit the underside of the object again. She needed to breathe. She needed to get out.

Suddenly, another underwater eddy tossed her around and around. She tumbled head over stinger so fast she didn't know which was up or down. Then, like something inedible, she was spat to the surface. She was about to go under again when she saw a long, twisting shadow not too far from her, a branch. She reached out and clung on to one of its lesser twigs, gasping and coughing as she floated downstream with it.

After a moment or two, feeling a little better, Samantha searched for her friend. Apart from the occasional flash of lightning, it was incredibly dark.

117

There wasn't much she could see apart from the branch. Several times she called out for Lizzie without reply, then gave up. It was no use. She just hoped and prayed that Lizzie had found purchase on a log or branch like she had done. Then, summoning her last reserves of energy, she dragged her exhausted body out of the water to a higher and drier section of the branch. Safe from the rushing water, she nestled into a small hollow and collapsed, utterly worn out, into a deep slumber.

Hours later, when she stirred, she discovered that the branch had become stuck on a sandbank. The river was now calm and serene. The skies, too, had calmed, blue with a dash of white, as if the storm had never happened. She tried flapping her wings, but they were tied. Along with finding her friend, cutting the rope was one of the first things she would have to do.

She climbed down to the end of the branch to where it rested on the riverbank and called for Lizzie, scanning the bending shoreline. Debris was everywhere – logs, branches, and what appeared to be a tattered portrait of Procruste Ant. Just as she was about to call again, Samantha heard someone shouting her name. She spun around to see Mad Jack coming toward her, waving his spade.

They met halfway, both glad the other was safe, and quickly exchanged their version of what had happened during the night. He had escaped arrest by jumping into the river, just before the storm hit, and had been waiting at the river bend as they'd planned, digging some holes to pass the time.

"Then I heard you shout for Miss McCoon," he said, "and saw you near that log."

Samantha wanted to know if he'd seen Lizzie, but Mad Jack shook his head. "We need to find her," she said, her wings sagging. "But first of all, I want this rope off me." She turned to show him her shackles. "If I can fly, I can cover a lot of area."

Mad Jack obliged, but the water had caused the knots to tighten and they were impossible to untie. The rope was also too tough for his maws. Even the edge of his spade couldn't cut it.

"Maybe we should go back to the anthills then," Samantha said, sighing. "If Lizzie washed ashore, she'd probably do the same."

"I thought we were going to the lake," he said. "Isn't that why we escaped?"

He was right, of course. She was on a quest to find Beebylon and her Bee Dream. Everything had happened to point her in that direction – the sunflowers, the ants, the storm – it would be foolish to go back. She had to keep following the omens, and maybe along the way she would find Lizzie, too. Their destinies were somehow linked, that she could feel, and the lake had something to do with it.

WITH RENEWED ENTHUSIASM, she began the slow trek downstream. She kept to the riverbank for most of the day, weaving around the flotsam and jetsam tossed by the storm, scrambling over, and sometimes under, the larger logs and pieces of wood. Mad Jack would often stop to dig a hole. Around noon, she found a flywheel lying in and out of the river. Next to it was a sign: THROUGH SEWING COMES FREEDOM, confirming her worst fears.

Suddenly, the sandy bank rippled beneath her feet. She jumped back. The sand caved in at the spot where she'd just been standing, and Mad Jack popped his head out. "Where are we?" he asked, blinking in the bright light. "Are we at the lake?"

Gazing downstream, Samantha shook her head, not knowing how far they were; she couldn't see further than the pines. "You almost scared me half to death," she said, her heart still fast from the shock. "Why are you tunneling, anyway?"

Mad Jack shrugged, holding his spade. "I figured it'd increase my chances of finding honeyroot," he said. "Don't worry about me. As long as you keep to the riverbank, I'll keep up." Then he disappeared in a spray of sand.

The trek was long and difficult. For the rest of the day, Samantha kept to the shadows of the pines, always in sight of the river. Mad Jack was somewhere underground and there was still no sign of Lizzie. She was beginning to wonder when, if ever, she would get to the lake. Then, lost in thought, she stepped out of the shadows and into the warmth of the late afternoon sun. There, before her very eyes, cupped in a forested valley, was a sea of blue.

"The lake," she whispered with awe.

It was just as she had imagined. For a wonderful moment, she believed she had stumbled upon the fabled Gardens of the Great Mother. She saw pine-covered slopes. She saw the sunflower field. She saw a waterfall spilling down the face of a cliff, and at its base a magnificent rainbow arching from shore to shore. If Beebylon existed at all, then it surely existed here.

The lapping waters drew her attention to her feet. A bottle of ant-perfume had been washed ashore. She picked it up and read the engraving: LIZZIE McCOON. SPECIAL CITIZEN SECOND CLASS. Her antennae stiffened. She quickly scanned for her friend. Only pines, frustratingly, and a sign nailed to

120

a trunk, old and faded and difficult to read. She didn't even see Mad Jack. She called for Lizzie but there was no reply, only the twitter of a blackbird somewhere in the treetops.

The perfume bottle slipped from her grip and she held back a tear. She should have listened to Lizzie. She should have stayed in the anthill, even if it wasn't her Bee Dream. No destiny was worth the death of a friend.

At that moment, she heard a mumble, like someone wakening from a deep sleep. "Lizzie?" she asked, facing left and right, then left and right again. "Where are you?"

The voice got louder. "Samantha! Up here!"

Samantha craned her neck and got a second fright. Lizzie was dangling upside down from a branch of a pine tree, her rear legs bound with twine. Her overalls looked a little worse for wear and all her perfume bottles had fallen off. She was as high as the first set of branches, too high for her to reach.

"What are you doing up there?" she asked.

"What does it look like?" Lizzie said. "I've been snared!"

Samantha followed the twine to the ground, where it was looped around a wooden peg. "I'll have you down in a jiffy," she said, walking to the peg.

Just as she bent down to unravel the knot, she heard a *snap!* then a *whoosh!* Something whipped past her face, like a tautly bent branch flicking straight. Then a sinewy claw grabbed her legs and ripped her off her feet. She screamed, surprised and shocked at the same time, and within the flap of a wing she was dangling upside down next to Lizzie, a loop of twine around her feet.

"That's just great!" Lizzie said. "Now we're both stuck. What'll we do now?" She furiously scratched an itch on one of her legs. "We're going to die," she moaned, now scratching her cheek, "upside down, like a spider. Why did I ever agree to come with you? I had a good life before I met you." Lizzie stopped scratching and glared at Samantha. "And don't you dare tell me this has happened for a reason! The only reason *is* we're going to die."

It was a moment before Samantha gathered her senses. She spied the sign on the tree she'd seen earlier. Though upside down, she was still able to read it: TRESPASSERS PROSECUTED. BY ORDER OF PRINCE ROBBEE (ON BEHALF OF QUEEN BEELINDA).

Lizzie pointed to something she had seen on the shore. "Did you see that? The sand moved." She reached for her belt, but there were no bottles. "I don't like it," she said. "Something's coming, something big. It's going to eat us. We're going to die!"

Samantha saw it instantly. A part of the shore collapsed into a small hole. From her position, it looked as though a hole had been poked into a golden sky. There was a spray of sandy rain before Mad Jack popped his head out, blinking in the sunshine.

"Samantha, where are you?" he asked, looking this way and that. "Are we at the lake yet?"

Lizzie stared down at him, momentarily stunned. "What's *he* doing here?" she asked.

Mad Jack craned his neck. He looked just as surprised to see Lizzie. "What are *you* doing up there?" he asked.

"We're trapped," Samantha said. "Would you mind helping us down?"

"Anything to help two maidens in distress," he said, grinning. Using his spade to prop himself up, he clambered out of his hole. Then he bowed. "Your hero to the rescue!"

"We don't need a hero," Lizzie said, scratching another facial itch. "Quit blabbering and get us down from these stupid traps."

Mad Jack said nothing. At the peg around which Samantha's twine was wound, he reached down to untie the knot. They all heard a *snap!* and a *whoosh!* There was a blur of white, and before Samantha could yell out a warning, Mad Jack was dangling upside down next to her. His spade fell from his grip, clanging to the ground beneath him.

"That's just *marvelous*," Lizzie said, gaping with disbelief. "Now we'll never get down. What kind of hero are *you*?"

Mad Jack stared despondently at the ground.

"Now, now. Let's not put the blame on anyone for our situation," Samantha said. "Let's think about what we can do."

Except for some grumbled mutterings from Lizzie, an awkward silence fell over the captives. It lasted for the rest of the evening. They watched the sun sink behind the waterfall, a huge orange ball that briefly set the sky on fire. Then the moon and stars came out, twinkling and reflecting off the dark, still waters of the lake; and as the night grew even darker, they heard whooping and howling coming from somewhere in the woods. It sent shivers down Samantha's wings, but as the moon began to set the howls drifted away and there was nothing save the silence of the night.

As sleep overcame her, Samantha again heard Lizzie muttering they were going to die. She didn't reply, secretly dreading the very same thing. If hunger or thirst didn't kill them, then who- or *what*-ever set these traps surely would.

SAMANTHA HEARD A noise as she slept, the snapping of a twig. It was soon followed by the sound of approaching footsteps. She blinked awake to the new, upside down morning, and was surprised to see seven of the largest bees she had ever seen directly beneath. One stood apart from the rest, the one from whom the others seemed to be waiting orders. He was tall and handsome, and try as she might, Samantha couldn't take her eyes off him.

"Well, well, well," he said, staring up. His smile was reminiscent of Gerald The Great, large and inviting. "What have our traps caught here?" He turned to one of his companions. "It looks like our little hunting party has caught three trespassers."

"Aye, Prince Robbee," the other bee said, also smiling. "That it does."

Samantha's jaw dropped open. Royalty! She suddenly became very self-conscious. Did she look all right? Were her antennae straight? It was just her luck to actually meet a prince when she had just woken up and looked a right mess. Worse, she was upside down! It couldn't be more embarrassing.

"And what should we do with them?" the prince asked, looking up again.

Out of the corner of her eyes, Samantha saw Lizzie and Mad Jack stirring. She quickly found her voice. "Please, sir," she said. "We didn't know we were trespassing. If you'll just let us down, we'll be on our way."

"A fair deal for a fair maiden," the prince said, still smiling. She kind of liked his unusual accent. "But let us not be hasty. Before I decide whether or not to let you go, I'd hear more of what you were doing on royal grounds without permission. It should make for interesting listening."

Chuckling, the hunting party set about lowering Samantha to the ground, then Lizzie and Mad Jack, and untied the twine from their feet. Free from her bonds, Samantha craned her neck to look into the prince's face. It was only now, standing side-by-side, that she fully comprehended his and the others' size. She was a little daunted. They were at least twice as big as she was, even bigger than a bumblebee. It was best to tell him the truth, which she did.

The prince considered her story. "I know of no ants and no anthill upstream," he said, glancing at the river. "But it does explain the bizarre clothes you're wearing and the rope around your wings. Here, turn around. Let me untie you."

Samantha turned her back to Prince Robbee. She could feel his large claws unpicking the tight knots, liking the romantic idea of being rescued by a prince. Within a minute, she was free. She flapped her wings, slowly at first, then more vigorously as the stiffness worked its way out. Before she knew it, her feet were hovering above the ground. It felt good to buzz again. It had been too long.

To her surprise, Samantha felt Prince Robbee grab her waist and pull her back down. "I'm afraid you can't do that," he said, suddenly serious, though Samantha detected a touch of sadness in his voice. "Flying's forbidden in the queendom."

Samantha glanced at Lizzie, who just shrugged. Behind her, at the edge of the woods, Mad Jack had already picked up his spade and begun digging a hole. The rest of the hunting party were resetting the traps. "Why do you have laws that stop you from being a bee?" Samantha asked, remembering

125

what Lizzie had once said about the laws in her hive. "How can you gather nectar? How does your hive survive? And forgive me for asking, but what kind of bee are you?"

The smile returned to the prince's handsome face. "So many questions," he said. "But if you're truly interested in finding the answers to them all, why don't you and your companions accompany my hunting party back to the hive? We can give you shelter and food, and it's only a day's trek from here. If we leave now, we should arrive before sunset. Consider it a royal invitation."

"And where, exactly, is your hive?" Lizzie asked, scratching her side.

The prince pointed westward. "Do you see the cliff and the waterfall?" he asked. "Our hive is there. My mother is the queen. Her name is Queen Beelinda. My father is King Bernard. We call the hive, Beebylon. Perhaps you've heard of it?"

Samantha's eyes blinked wide. She could barely believe it. Only last evening she had been hanging upside down in the trap, despairing of her fate. Now, in such a short space of time, her luck had completely reversed. She was filled with hope and anticipation that grew with every beat of her heart. Mad Jack had stopped digging and was winking at her.

"I certainly have," she said to the prince.

WITHOUT FURTHER ADO, the prince led the way along the shore toward Beebylon. Samantha was at his side, something she found not too displeasing. As the sun lifted above the pine tops and began to shine directly down upon them, Lizzie and the hunting party fell someway back, chatting and laughing amongst themselves. Mad Jack though, Samantha noticed, had disappeared somewhere, presumably beneath the sand.

As they walked, Samantha began to feel more at ease with the prince. Though their progress was too slow for her liking, her eagerness to get to Beebylon was almost forgotten in his presence. She plucked the courage to tell him more of herself. She spoke of her trial and expulsion from the hive, hoping he wouldn't think too unkindly of her, and how she had met Lizzie and the quest they embarked upon, to find their destiny at the lake. By the time she had finished, the cliff loomed large, casting its shadow upon them.

"You asked me before what kind of bees we are," the prince said, pausing for a moment. The lake rippled in a gentle breeze. "Carpenter bees, masters of woodcraft. At least we were, in a time long forgotten. Our ancestors came from a land far, far away. It's said from even beyond the rising sun. We've kind of kept the traditional way of life, making our nests in tunnels. But unlike our great ancestors, who generally liked the solitary way of life, we've chosen to live in community with other bees." A heavy sadness now seemed to weigh down on him. "You're probably wondering why it's forbidden to fly in the queendom," he said. "It's a tragedy we rarely speak of. When my father was a young prince, he suffered a terrible accident. A great gust of wind, as often happens around Beebylon, threw him onto the rocks at the base of the cliff. It greatly disfigured his wings. He's been unable to fly ever since."

Samantha felt for the king. It wasn't natural to be permanently grounded. She had had glimpses of it during her time in Hive Prison and the anthill, but that had only been temporary. To never fly for the rest of her life would probably drive her crazy.

"A great darkness fell over my father's mind," the prince continued. "My grandmother, who was the queen of the hive back then, passed a law forbidding all other bees to fly. She hoped he wouldn't be reminded of his failings. Now, as the years have passed, only the most elderly can recall what it was like to buzz around the fields and the gardens."

As he finished speaking, Samantha noticed the sand rippling up ahead. It collapsed into a small hole and out popped Mad Jack's head. He turned this way and that, then halted when he saw them approaching. "Are we there yet?" he asked.

"Less than two more hours, I should say," the prince said, somewhat bemused. Mad Jack nodded and disappeared in a spray of sand. The prince peered into the hole. "Why does he dig so much?"

"He's searching for honeyroot," Samantha said. "He wants to turn stone into honey."

The prince suddenly burst out laughing, his claw on his belly. He laughed and laughed and laughed, and it was a while before he could even speak. By then, Lizzie and the hunting party had caught up with them. When Prince Robbee told them what Samantha had said, they all burst out laughing too. Samantha glared at him.

"What is it?" the prince asked. "You don't find it amusing? He's searching for something that doesn't exist."

"I was also told that Beebylon didn't exist," she said, and walked away, her claws clenched. At least Mad Jack was trying to find his destiny, she said to herself. Didn't anyone believe in searching for a dream?

Secretly, however, she was worried. If honeyroot didn't exist in Beebylon, then it didn't exist any-where.

SAMANTHA, LIZZIE, MAD JACK, the prince and his hunting party followed the steady rise of the shoreline, now rocky and slippery, until it abruptly ended at the cliff. Samantha guessed they had climbed less than a quarter up the face. Surprisingly, it was riddled with pockets no bigger than her parents' hive-cell. There were thousands of them. The cliff seemed more air than rock.

Left side, the waterfall rushed to the lake below, where a beautiful rainbow arched through the mist like a gateway to hive-heaven. Samantha followed the waterfall up the cliff. It climbed high above, way, way up toward the heavens, much higher than even the tallest trees in the woods. The very sky seemed to sit on it, a blue ceiling atop a brown wall. How she wished the law forbidding flight could be re-voked. How she wished she could fly to the top and see the view from up there. She imagined it would be quite magnificent.

"Welcome to Beebylon," shouted Prince Robbee above the noise of the waterfall. "I'm sure you'll just love it here."

It was the arrival Samantha had dreamed of. She was here. She was *really* here, at Beebylon, the magical hive where everyone was rich and where honey dripped from the walls. She looked over her wings. Lizzie was staring up at the top of the waterfall, scratching her cheek and seemingly in awe. Mad Jack, too, unable to dig in the rocks but still with his spade, was staring up. She could tell he was excited at finally arriving. It was just as she felt.

The prince led them through the mist onto a slender ledge that took them into a large, hidden cavern behind the waterfall. It was darker and a lot quieter inside. The ledge they were on continued along the wall and disappeared into the darkness at the back of the cavern. Dozens more ledges above, and several below, were alive with movement, bees hurrying to and fro, somewhat reminiscent of the central bee-way in her old hive.

"This ledge is called the Honey Way," the prince said. "The main ledge above is called the Field of Lilies. It's the main tourist route. It's also where the palace is."

As they continued down the Honey Way, Samantha noticed that the cavern walls were pitted with thousands of smaller caves, just like the cliff face. So too the roof, which stretched high, high above. Sunlight streamed through the holes onto the floor, scattering white specks upon it like stars at night on the lake. Samantha was captivated. Beebylon was more magical than she had ever imagined. With each step she was more and more certain that this was the place where her dreams would come true.

"Vermin!" someone shouted nearby. "No good vermin!"

Up ahead, a bee staggered along the ledge clasping a lavender sac to his chest. He had exited from one of the many caves, above which was a sign: THE ROSE AND THORN. The bee lifted a clenched claw and shouted at them again. "Lock 'em up!" he said, staggering back. He took a swig from the lavender sac and wiped his mouth with the back of his claw. "No good vermin!"

"Damn lavender," the prince muttered. "It makes them all drunk. Just ignore him."

Samantha tried her best, but the drunkard kept shouting. Her hive had its share of down-and-outs, too, but she never thought she would see bees like this in Beebylon.

The drunkard then said something horrible about the prince's father. "Be quiet!" the prince said. "Or you'll find yourself behind bars."

"Ah, yar mother was a weevil!" the drunkard shouted in return, then staggered back and fell over. He didn't get up.

Samantha was shocked to hear the prince being spoken to like that. In her hive, the drunkard would have been sent to the dungeons and never seen again, but the prince didn't want to waste his energy. He told Samantha and the others to continue along the ledge, where they passed another tavern smelling of stale lavender and vomit. From inside they could hear a kind of sick, tuneless hum and someone yelling abuse at the waiter. One of the drunkards threw an empty lavender sac through the door, striking Lizzie on the side of her head.

"Just my luck!" she mumbled, rubbing the spot where it had hit.

Samantha was stumped. What, in hive-heaven, was going on? This was supposed to be her Bee Dream, but every third or fourth cave was abandoned or rundown, the rest of them lavender taverns or places of ill repute. Moreover, almost every step of the way, bees pleaded for honey, even honeydew, some of them so desperate they threw themselves at the prince's feet. Garbage, too, was piled in stinking heaps. It beggared belief. A darkness of spirit had descended on Beebylon like a curse. Nobody was rich. Nobody was happy. And honey certainly wasn't dripping from the walls.

Further on, the prince ushered them into a side tunnel with stairs chiseled into the rock face. They climbed several ledges to the Field of Lilies. "Please forgive the rudeness of some of my fellow bees," he said, as Samantha exited onto the ledge. "Beebylon isn't the hive it used to be."

Though in slightly better condition than below, the caves on the Field of Lilies were still rundown and in poor condition. She just nodded and kept her thoughts to herself.

"As you can see," Prince Robbee said, sighing, "the hive is struggling terribly. Beebylon was once beautiful, its riches the envy of every bee in the known world. They used to say that honey dripped from these very walls, that we'd discovered the secret to Infinite Richness. Alas, those days are now long gone. Beebylon is crumbling before our very eyes, for one simple reason – we've forgotten how to fly. We've forgotten how to be a bee. If it continues for much longer, I fear Beebylon will be abandoned."

Samantha was aghast at the very thought of it. For a hive, there could be no worse fate than abandonment, but if it should happen to Beebylon...

"Perhaps I can be of some assistance," she said, not dwelling on an outcome that hadn't yet arrived. It was better to think positively, and not let the situation weigh her down. She had to help, that much she knew, in any way she could. "I was a pupil at aerobatic flying school. I can teach you how to buzz and fly. It's not that difficult once you know how."

"Alas, it's not that simple." Prince Robbee sighed again. "The problem is a legal issue. Once a law is made it cannot be revoked, otherwise my mother would've done it a long time ago. Until my father can fly, no bee is allowed to buzz or flap her wings. And if he should die before…" He let that thought slide, then said, "It's an impossible solution."

"It's not impossible," Samantha said, already planning how to solve the problem. "Some things at first seem like a dark hole, but you can always avoid a void. All you need is the proper position of your apposition." Glancing at the ceiling, watching the streams of sunlight through the holes, she told the prince of her encounter with Gerald The Great. "The first step is to build some new wings for the king," she then said. "The question is, how?"

"Aye, Samantha, how?" the prince asked. "It's a question not even the brightest minds in Beebylon can answer. Why do you think you can succeed?"

"Because if everything happens for a reason, there has to be a Reason Giver, someone who is in ultimate control," she said. "I now know why the Great Mother has brought me here to Beebylon. To help your father fly."

THE GROUP ARRIVED at the palace. It was larger than any of the caves Samantha had so far seen inside Beebylon. A dozen guards stood to attention out-side, large carpenter bees that towered over her like the prince. "We call the palace, Honeyrood," the prince said. "I do hope you'll feel at home."

Samantha, Lizzie and Mad Jack were escorted past the guards and down several winding corridors that tunneled deeper into the cavern wall. Saman-tha wondered how the carpenter bees could dig into rock. She was reminded of the tunnels inside the anthill, though where they had been whitewashed and adorned with portraits of Procruste Ant, these tunnels were barefaced rock covered with silky green drapes and portraits of stern-looking kings and queens with names she'd never heard of. The corridors were also higher and wider than in the anthill, presumably to accommodate the greater, physical size of the carpenter bees. Samantha passed many rooms behind closed doors, and many statuettes and busts of more unknown kings and queens.

The prince then showed Samantha, Lizzie and Mad Jack to their chambers, three adjacent bed-cells along one of the corridors. Samantha couldn't help but notice the quality of craftwork in her room – the luxurious four-posted bed, the ornately carved frame on the queen's portrait, the imposing wooden dressing table – even she could tell they were the work of highly skilled carpenters. Though a thin coating of dust covered everything, the wealth that had once existed in Beebylon was obvious. If only she could help the king to fly again. Then the law forbidding flight would be revoked and Beebylon would once again rise to majestic heights.

The prince told her to put her feet up and relax for a while. Someone would be along to collect her in an hour. He was excited to discuss her plan of building wings for the king. "And there's no need to wear those overalls," he said. "You're not a captive of the ants anymore. You're a guest of the queen of Beebylon."

Barely a minute after the prince and his hunting party left, Samantha heard a knock on her door. Lizzie popped her head in, scratching an itch on her cheek. "Do you have a moment? I need to have a word with you."

"Sure," Samantha said. "What's the problem?"

"What's the problem?" Lizzie said, entering and shutting the door. "Are you joking? This place is a dump." She spread four of her arms out wide. "Look at this room, everything's covered in dust. It's just like the rest of Beebylon. The whole place is run-down. I didn't leave everything behind for this."

Samantha removed her overalls and sat on the edge of the bed. "What do you want us to do? Go back to what we were doing before we met?"

"It was better in the anthill," Lizzie said, wiping her claw along the dressing table. It left a thin streak in the dust.

"I know what you're afraid of. You always get worried and scared every time you're going to molt," Samantha said. "It's the last time, too, isn't it? Then you're going to pupate. You're afraid be-cause it's something you can't control."

Lizzie stopped running her claw over the dusty tabletop. "Well, I guess I'm not as perfect as Miss Samantha B. Honeycomb who never gets scared at anything."

Samantha felt her wings prickle with anger. She remained silent for a moment, not wanting to say something she would regret later. "I get scared all the time. I wouldn't be a bee if I didn't," she said. "I just try not to let fear dictate what I should or should not do."

"Then how do you overcome it?" Lizzie asked, absently scratching her side.

"If my path is clouded with fear or anger, I pray to the Great Mother to guide me through until it clears," Samantha said.

"And what do you think the Great Mother wants us to do now?" Lizzie asked.

"Your path is your path," Samantha said, matter of fact. "I cannot tell you what to do. All I know is that the Great Mother wants you to be the best caterpillar you can be. You know in your heart what that is. Whether or not you allow the Great Mother to guide you is up to you. As for me, I believe She has led us here for a reason, to help the king to fly. The prince will be calling for us in less than an hour to discuss further plans. You have until then to decide if you want to be a part of it."

Lizzie then left to go back to her room and think about what Samantha had said, scratching one of her legs as she went.

WITHIN THE HOUR, as arranged, a palace servant came to escort them to the prince's chamber. Samantha was glad when Lizzie stepped out of her bed-cell. She was also surprised to see she was no longer wearing her overalls. Mad Jack, however, was still wearing his. At the end of the corridor, they arrived at a set of double doors. Two guards stood to attention outside it and allowed them entry.

The prince's room was like Samantha's, only bigger and grander, with more silky drapes and portraits and statuettes, and a four-posted bed that was at least twice as big. The prince was sitting behind a large desk. On top of the desk was a bunch of scrolls and some pencils. He stood and greeted the guests, wasting no time in getting down to work.

"Before you tell me your plans, let me show you one of my own designs," he said, unrolling one of the scrolls. "As you can see, it's in the shape of a bee. The pilot sits in the abdomen section and uses

136

levers to flap the wings." Then he stopped, just sighing at the drawing. "Alas, it failed to get off the ground, just like all the other ones we built."

He unrolled several more scrolls. All the designs, Samantha saw, were one variation or another of the first. "The main problem we're facing is weight," he said. "The pilot can't flap fast enough to get off the ground. We make all the prototypes out of Bee-bylonian honeywood, which is exactly the type of wood you need to build a flying machine, light and strong, but even then it's too heavy. We don't know where to go next. We're just going round and round in circles. It's all amounted to nothing."

Something is nothing and nothing is something, Gerald The Great had said. "It's not completely no-thing," Samantha said. The prince looked up from his scrolls. "You've eliminated several options. That's at least something."

"What do you propose, then?" he asked.

"The proper position of our apposition." She pointed high toward the ceiling. "Kite gliding!" she said.

All eyes turned up to where she was pointing, then returned. The prince's expression was blank. "What, may I ask, is a kite?"

"A flying machine," Samantha said. "One that's so light it can glide on currents of air. All it requires is for the wind to blow. Its wings are fixed, so it needs no levers to flap, or anything else for that matter. I believe it'll solve the problems you've been facing." She stepped right up to the desk. "Let me show you what I mean."

Samantha asked the prince to unroll a blank scroll and grabbed a pencil. She then sketched a diagram of the kite she had seen flying outside the hive, the same one she had also examined the day she was escorted to the Crazy Lands. It was a simple design, a wing-sheet made of light material that would be cut into a diamond and fixed upon a frame of crossing wooden beams. The king would hang beneath the kite in a harness made from Samantha's overalls and fixed to the crossbeams. As an added precaution, the kite would be tethered to a pulley mechanism so that it couldn't fly away.

"There will have to be test flights, of course," she said, "before it's safe for the king."

The prince nodded thoughtfully.

"He won't buzz through the forest like he did before the...." She didn't dare say the dreaded word. "But all things considered," she said, "it's probably the king's best chance of ever flying again."

Samantha put the pencil down. All agreed that it was a mighty fine proposal. The prince was sure King Bernard would be delighted, and would seek his immediate counsel. Nothing could go ahead until he and the queen gave their royal approval, so with Samantha's scroll of the new flying machine in his grasp, Prince Robbee led Samantha, Lizzie and Mad Jack down several corridors to the throne room. He harried ahead of them, eager to tell the king of the new plan.

Samantha followed, nervous at the prospect of meeting the king and queen. After all, her last encounter with a monarch hadn't ended so well, had it? She had to keep reminding herself that she hadn't broken any laws of this hive.

Nonetheless, she still felt intimidated: experience had taught her that the unexpected could occur at anytime, anywhere.

THEY ARRIVED AT a set of high double doors, outside which stood four guards. The prince pushed past them and burst into the throne room without waiting to be announced.

"Father!" he said, holding the scroll aloft. "I have the answer we've been looking for."

Samantha and her friends entered behind him, awe-struck. The throne room was as opulent as anything she had seen. The high vaulted ceiling, the two grandiose thrones, the servants (almost as motionless as the statues of kings and queens lining the walls), the waxed floors that reflected her face like the still surface of the lake, it was just as she imagined the most important chamber in the whole of Beebylon should be. It was a little overwhelming, actually.

Upon the thrones sat Queen Beelinda and King Bernard, muted and unsmiling. Though the queen sat proudly, her back straight, her head held high, the king looked weak and frail. He struggled to keep his head aloft, as though it was made of rock. Bent forward, he gripped the armrests to prevent himself from toppling off. The prince was right, Samantha mused. The plan had to succeed, and soon.

Prince Robbee strode across the wide floor to the thrones, unrolling the scroll as he went. He explained the design and the technical details to the king and queen, who listened patiently, nodding almost imperceptibly now and then, waiting until their son had finished everything he wanted to say.

"All we need is your blessing," the prince said.

The king seemed troubled by a thought. When he finally lifted his heavy head to speak, his voice was slow and strained. "Who will operate this... this kite, as you call it?" he asked.

The prince was about to answer. "I'll pilot it," said Samantha, stepping forward. She'd been ready for that question. "It's my design. If something should happen during the test flight, it's my responsibility."

A faint smile flickered on the old face. "You will need materials," the king said.

Samantha had spent the time in her bed-cell preparing a mental list of what she would need. She told the queen and king that Mad Jack would collect honeywood for the frame, and with their permission, she would use silk from the palace for the wing-sheet. What they couldn't get in Beebylon they could get from the ants. Lizzie would go as she had the best relationship with them.

"We'll also need some honey," Samantha said. "The ants won't even think of trading without it."

Head still bent forward, the king looked at the queen. A silent communication passed between the two. "Beebylon isn't as rich as it once was," the queen then said. "The last of our honey reserves ran out last year. We're virtually bankrupt."

The situation was direr than Samantha had reckoned. "Don't worry," she said. "We'll just have to think of a way to make a trade without honey."

"My hunting party will accompany Lizzie, just in case," the prince said. "We don't want the ants to arrest her again. She'll be safe."

Samantha nodded. It was a good idea. Next to her, Lizzie was scratching an itch on her abdomen. There was only one last thing to organize. "Prince Robbee, you and I shall be responsible for the main construction of the flying machine," she said. "Your skills as a carpenter are vital. It cannot be built without you."

Prince Robbee smiled, and the force of his gaze caught Samantha by surprise. "My dear damsel, it cannot be built without *you*."

He then thanked his parents and bade them goodnight. Though only just detectable, Samantha could feel the heavy sense of despair lifting from the room as he escorted her, Lizzie and Mad Jack out into the corridor. The smile on the prince's face was with him every step of the way back to their bed-cells, as if all his Great Mother Days had come at once.

"Tomorrow," he said at Samantha's door, "we begin construction on a magnificent flying machine."

THE NEXT DAY, Prince Robbee gained the queen's approval for the requisition of an abandoned cave high upon the cliff, an old hiveware factory that had fallen upon hard times. The cave was ideal for the assembly of the flying machine, spacious, dry and hidden from prying eyes. It also had a view across the lake that was simply stunning. The prince posted a dozen guards at the entrance with orders that only he, Samantha, Lizzie, and Mad Jack were allowed entry. The building of the kite was top secret.

For the next week, they busied themselves with the tasks they had been assigned. Lizzie left immediately with the hunting party to trade with the ants. Mad Jack went in search of honeywood, after the prince explained what to look for, the shape and color of the leaves, the texture of the bark, its size ("They grow no taller than the height of this ceiling inside the factory," he said), and instructed him on the use of an axe. Mad Jack told them not to worry;

he would get what they needed. Then he went missing for three days.

In the meantime, Samantha and the prince set to work designing the specifics of the flying machine and making small models from bits of materials lying in and around the cave, tasks that took longer than she had reckoned upon.

"You seem to know so much about flying," the prince said on the third afternoon.

Samantha waved away his compliment, flushing coyly, which, she noticed, was becoming more and more of a regularity whenever the prince was near. His presence seemed to make her claws tremble and her wings flutter, like a little grub falling hopelessly antennae over stinger in love with a famous celebrity. Why was she like this? Was it his looks: his height, his strength, his attractive eyes and smile? Or was it his enthusiasm to make life better for his subjects? Or was it simply because he was the prince of Beebylon, straight out of a fairytale?

The prince picked up the model of the kite they had just completed (they'd finally got it right on the seventh try), turning it over front and back. "Are you sure it'll fly?" he asked. "I'm worried for your safety when you take it for a test flight. I don't want the same thing to happen to you as it did my father."

Samantha eyed the model flying machine. It had every detail – diamond-shaped wing-sheet, wooden crossbeams, hanging harness – and although she had a nagging sense that something was missing, she was more than happy with the result.

"Did you know that it's theoretically impossible for a bumblebee to fly?" she said. "But they do. Isn't that amazing?"

She glanced up, and was once again struck at the force of his gaze. "Aye, amazing it is," he said.

"It's also amazing that you are completely unaware of your beauty."

Now she did blush. She could feel her cheeks burn, as if she had sat too close to a campfire, and her claws began to tremble again. "I... I... I must go and check on the material for the wing-sheet," she said, and went to the back of the cave.

She spent the rest of the day sorting through the boxes of silk drapes the prince had ordered, some she recognized as coming straight from the very corridors of Honeyrood. She examined every strip of material, meticulously checking for holes or signs of weakness, but she knew she was overdoing it. She was simply avoiding contact with the prince. What was happening? Her emotions were soaring. Worse, she had no control over them, like she'd been lifted to the heavens on a sudden gust of wind and now couldn't get back down.

It was better not to think about it, so she returned to sorting the same silk drapes over and over again. The prince was at the mouth also pretending to be busy, toying with the model kite. To her relief, Mad Jack arrived that evening with a bundle of wood on his back. She saw him glance from her to the prince, then back again, cocking his antennae, and felt her face begin to flush once more.

"I found some honeywood trees on the other side of the lake," he said, setting the bundle down at the entrance. There was a strange glint in his eyes. "I need help to bring the bigger pieces back. They're too heavy."

"Let me see what you've got," the prince said, dropping the model and hurrying over. "Aye, it's perfect. Light and strong. Look Samantha."

She came over and examined the wood, but not before sharing a quick, tentative glance with the prince. "Well done," she said to Mad Jack. "Maybe the prince can organize for one of his servants to help you collect the rest."

"That won't be necessary," the prince said. "I will go with Mad Jack myself." He laid a friendly arm on Mad Jack's shoulder. "But let's wait for the morrow. It's been a long day. We need to rest and eat and regain our strength."

THAT EVENING AFTER Samantha had supped with the king and queen and kept them updated on the progress so far, she received a knock on her bed-cell door. For a moment she thought Lizzie had returned from the anthill, until Mad Jack popped his head in and asked to see her. Before he entered, he scanned both directions down the corridor, then quickly shut the door and, to Samantha's surprise, locked it. He was also without his spade.

"I found it!" he said, hopping from one leg to the other, unable to contain himself. "I found it, Samantha! I actually found it!"

Samantha gestured for him to calm down. "What is it? What did you find?"

Mad Jack reached into the front pocket of his overalls and removed what looked to Samantha like nothing more than a small stone. "Honeyroot!" he whispered.

She took the stone from Mad Jack, who was rather reluctant to let go of it, and held it up to her eye. It was amber in color, the color of purest honey, and clear, like the waters of the lake, so clear in fact she could see Mad Jack's face when she looked through it. It was also weighty, though not as heavy as a rock or pebble of the same size.

"So this is honeyroot," she said, also whispering.

Mad Jack took his amber stone back. "No, this is what honeyroot does. It turns stone into honey, which is this, solidified honey," he said, continuing to admire it. "Think of it as honeystone, a gem. It's worth a fortune."

Samantha wondered if it were truly as valuable as Mad Jack believed. "Where d'you find it?" she asked.

"Where I should've looked all these years," he said, putting it back in his pocket. "At the roots of the honeywood tree."

Honeyroot. Honeywood. It suddenly made sense to Samantha, too.

"I don't know how it happens, all I know is that wherever honeywood trees grow, there's honeystone," Mad Jack said. "These carpenter bees don't know what a fortune is buried outside their cavern. They always chop a honeywood tree down and leave its roots alone, you see. I, on the other hand, found it difficult to use an axe. So I decided to do what I do best, dig! I discovered the honeystone at the base of the tree I was trying to fell. That's when the connection between honeyroot and honeywood hit me. I'm rich beyond my wildest dreams."

Samantha smiled. She smiled because her friend had had the courage to search for his dream against the odds and found it. She smiled because it was also a reminder never to give up hope in searching for what she believed in. And she smiled because now, armed with the knowledge of honeyroot and honeystone, she could finally return to her old hive and see her parents again.

But before then, she had a destiny to fulfill.

Five days after leaving, Lizzie and the hunting party returned from their expedition to the ant colony. Lizzie was different, somehow. Her skin looked shiny and new, and she was no longer scratching it. Behind her trailed a dozen or more ants carrying cardboard boxes on their back, which the prince instructed to be stored in a cave adjacent to the factory. Samantha recognized the leading ant as Lieutenant 7725695P, her security guard, and was a little wary.

Lizzie took her arm and led her to the back of the factory. Mad Jack was scratching around with his spade, testing the hardness of different spots on the walls and ground. His spade made annoying *chink!* *chink!* noises as it hit hard rock.

"There are soft spots in the cliff," he said as they approached. "These caves and tunnels must have been eroded by the wind and the water. I always wondered how it was possible to dig into rock."

Lizzie ignored him. "Don't look so worried," she whispered to Samantha, glancing at the ants. "The lieutenant's only here to do a trade. By the way, I had to promise them a lot more honey to bring the material here. They drive a hard bargain, you know. I hope you've managed to get some while I was away. They won't be happy to go back without any payment."

Samantha was at a loss. Her mind had been so busy (and not just with work, if she were being honest) she had forgotten all about the honey. What was she going to do? She stared at the ants, then back at Lizzie, her mind blank. It was impossible to think with all that noise from behind. The *chink!* *chink!* *chink!* of Mad Jack's spade was driving her up these rocky walls. Couldn't he do that some-where else?

"Mad Jack!" She shouted so loud her throat hurt. He immediately stopped. Then, as if his spade had chinked through a wall in her mind to reveal a hidden treasure, she suddenly saw what she need-ed to do. "Mad Jack," she said, her voice now sweet and calm. "I need something from you."

Samantha convinced him to part with three of his smallest honeystone gems. He was happy to on the proviso she talked with the prince on his behalf; he needed royal permission to claim a small plot of land where the honeywood grew. Samantha called the prince over and discussed the deal. The prince immediately agreed, claiming he would personally ensure the queen gave him the grant. Samantha wasn't sure the prince knew what he was giving away, but they needed Mad Jack's honeystones. It wasn't only the ants that could drive a hard bargain.

She handed the gems to the lieutenant and began to explain what they were.

"Honeystone!" he said, and sprayed a delightful perfume of vanilla and rose. "Can you believe it? Our splendiferous leader, the magnificent Procruste Ant will be ecstatic." He looked up at Samantha and Lizzie. "If you should require anything else, please don't hesitate to ask. We're more than happy to establish new trading partners, especially when they pay as prompt and as much as you."

With relief, Samantha watched the ants leave. "How were things at the anthill?" she asked Lizzie.

"They're still rebuilding what was damaged by the floods, but they seem in good spirits," Lizzie said. "Almost everyone made it to high ground and survived. They'll be back to normal soon enough."

Lizzie then showed Samantha what they'd been able to acquire from the anthills, opening all the boxes in the adjacent cave, now storeroom. "I'm afraid we could only get poor-grade cotton," Lizzie said, showing some of it to Samantha. "It's all they could spare. And we'll have to make do with assembling a spinning wheel from spare parts as well." She peered into another box and rummaged around. She looked distraught. "They could only give us scraps of denim, too. I'm sorry, Samantha, there's virtually nothing."

Something is nothing and nothing is something, Samantha thought. "We'll just have to make do with what we've got," she said. "We'll patch everything together."

Soon thereafter, the real work began on the construction of the flying machine. First, Samantha helped Lizzie reassemble the spinning wheel. Like the early days of their capture in the anthill, they took turns in spinning the cotton into thread. Then, with the sewing skills she learnt in Hive Prison, Samantha began stitching the scraps of denim into one large, patchwork sheet (she had made a last minute decision against using the palace silk, even though it was lighter; the denim was more durable and less likely to tear). The prince and Mad Jack went to collect more honeywood and to stake out Mad Jack's new plot of land. Samantha also wanted Prince Robbee, upon his return, to build a pulley mechanism large enough to anchor the kite during its flight, and in her spare time she sketched its design using the bobbin on the spinning wheel as a model for its construction.

The following evening Samantha was alone at the mouth of the factory cave. She was patching two pieces of denim together with needle and thread, gazing across the mirrored waters of the lake. She heard Lizzie approach from behind.

"You miss him, don't you?" Lizzie said.

"Who?" Samantha said, returning to her sewing. "I don't know what you mean."

Lizzie chuckled at her evasiveness. "You can't fool anyone, Samantha. We've all seen the look in your eyes when he's around. It's the same look he has for you, too."

Samantha kept silent, wondering if Lizzie was telling the truth.

"You always said that you'd find your Bee Dream at Beebylon," Lizzie said. "Maybe it's time you started believing your own words."

PRINCE ROBBEE AND Mad Jack arrived late the next morning carrying two logs of honeywood over their shoulders. Samantha greeted them, relieved that the prince had returned safely, but barely let him rest. She showed him the design of the pulley mechanism she wanted him to build, which, with Mad Jack's help, he set to straight away.

In the meantime, Samantha and Lizzie twined the cotton they had spun into rope, and two days later the pulley (essentially a large barrel mounted on supports) was completed. Under tight security, it was taken to the base of the cliff and guarded. Now it was time to assemble the kite.

Samantha instructed the prince and Mad Jack to lay one pole of honeywood across the other like a 't'. She then lashed them firmly together with one end of the rope she and Lizzie had twined, now many hundreds of yards long. When the poles were securely fastened, Samantha dropped the free end of the rope over the precipice and watched it fall to the base of the cliff. The prince was waiting for it. He gathered the rope and looped it around the barrel-pulley, like cotton spinning onto a bobbin.

Samantha, Lizzie and Mad Jack then mounted the patchwork wing-sheet onto the cross frame. They trimmed it and sewed it and lashed it securely, a task that took up most of the afternoon. The kite now had the shape of a large diamond. With the exception of its color and size, it was just like the kite she had seen flying in the field near her old hive.

"Now for the harness," she said to the others.

She made some simple adjustments to her old pair of overalls and secured it to the underside of the crossbeams. She had with her a loose knot of string she'd tied earlier. This she also secured to the crossbeams.

"What's that for?" Lizzie asked.

"You'll see," Samantha said. "Hopefully I'll never have to use it."

She, Lizzie, Mad Jack and the prince stood back to admire the flying machine. It was ready.

That night, they supped with the queen and king. Talk was of only one thing: the first test flight. Even the king seemed excited. He spoke of nothing else.

"It'll be just like the old days," he said, his face cracking into a smile. "We used to buzz through the forest and up to the top of the cliff. I even touched the clouds once."

"The clouds? Wow," Mad Jack said, with that dreamy look in his eyes.

The others laughed and the king winked coyly at Samantha, who said little, just content to listen and take joy at what she was hearing.

Hope.

PRINCE ROBBEE WOKE Samantha the next morning in her bed-cell earlier than normal and accompanied her and Lizzie to the factory cave. Eagerness and enthusiasm were shining from his eyes. Today was the big day, though most of the citizens of Beebylon were oblivious to what was about to happen. Samantha looked out through the mouth toward the sky. Large fluffy clouds drifted across the blue heavens. It was a perfect day for flying.

In the distance, a blackbird came swooping from the forest treetops toward the cliff. Samantha marveled at its skill in flight. She could see its magnificent feathers glisten in the morning sunshine. As it swooped by the cliff face, its long tail twitched ever so slightly and it turned in a majestic arc back to the pine trees. Its voice echoed across the lake: "Get up! Get up! Get up! The day is new. The sky is blue. Get up! Get up! Get up!"

Samantha took a deep breath. It was time. She checked the kite once over and made sure the overall-harness was fastened securely to the underside of the crossbeams.

"If something goes wrong," she said to Lizzie and the prince, grabbing the knot of string she had fixed yesterday, "I'll pull this release cord. I can then buzz safely to the ground."

Lizzie and Prince Robbee lifted the kite so that Samantha could slip into the harness. The prince remarked how light it was. Samantha slid the last strap over her shoulder and smiled at him, belying the tension that was gnawing at her belly like a hungry ant. "All right. Let's do it," she said.

While Lizzie and the prince held the kite, Samantha shuffled to the mouth of the cave and stood on the edge of the precipice. She peered down. The rope lashed to the central crossbeam ran all the way down the face of the cliff, tethering the kite to the barrel-pulley. Assembled next to it, Mad Jack, Queen Beelinda, King Bernard, six royal guards, and only the most trusted of the prince's hunting party, were staring up at her. Her heart was thumping and she suddenly felt moist and clammy inside the harness.

"There's no need to be so nervous," she told herself, whispering under her breath. "You can do it. Everything's going to be all right."

But she couldn't do it. It was such a long way down. It was far too dangerous. The temptation to step back and pull out was overwhelming. She glanced over her wings at her two friends, about to apologize that she couldn't go through with it, when the song she used to sing as a little grub suddenly hummed in her mind.

> *I am a little honeybee*
> *And Samantha is my name.*
> *I buzz and sing and laugh at things*
> *'Coz to me its all the same.*
>
> *I like to fly as high as crows*
> *Then dive into a rose.*
> *'Coz a honeybee is not afraid*
> *To bee what she is made.*

"Good luck," Lizzie said, and then unexpectedly leaned forward and rubbed Samantha's antennae.

The prince wished her luck, too; and to Samantha's surprise, he also rubbed her antennae.

It was just the encouragement she needed. She made a quick prayer for the Great Mother's blessing and jumped over the edge. She heard the kite rip from Lizzie and the prince's grip. For more than a horrid second, the kite dived straight toward the rocks below, but a gust of breeze picked it up and sent her soaring above the waterfall.

Suddenly, she felt a jolt. The rope tethered to the barrel-pulley had unwound to its end, anchoring her. This was the limit to which the kite could fly. She felt annoyed. She wanted to take it higher. She wanted to see how far this thing could really go. It had been so long since she had flown, she had forgotten what a joy it was.

Part of that joy was the feeling of peace. Part of it was the sense of freedom. A smaller part was physical, the wind through her antennae, the lightness of floating, even the unique view of the landscape from up high. Another thing she'd almost forgotten. It was as if the contours were drawn on a colorful, two-dimensional scroll – the blue waters stretching southward, the wiggling grey river down which she had escaped from the ants, the streak of golden sunflowers, the blur of green pines. There was more. Behind, far on the western horizon, the source of the waterfall emerged from a range of mountains she hadn't even known existed. From the base of the jagged peaks, the river sliced its way through valleys and forests before throwing itself over the edge of the cliff. What queendom, what mysteries, existed west of here? The world was far bigger than she'd ever imagined.

From below, she heard faint cheers and laughter coming to her on the updraft. Lizzie and the prince had rushed down and were waving at her, along with the rest of them, even the queen and king. Samantha waved back. She was doing it. She was really doing it.

She began singing her childhood song again when, unexpectedly, the wind changed direction. From a pleasant updraft, it flipped into a nasty downshift. The kite was ill prepared for such a sudden change. It plunged into a downward spiral. Round and round and round she went, twisting, twisting, twisting. She heard distant groans of horror from below. Instinctively, she grabbed hold of the crossbeam to control the plummet, but it made no difference. The kite kept spiraling like a leaf in a tornado.

"Pull the cord!" Prince Robbee yelled. His voice was faint and hard to hear. "Pull the cord!"

The rocky ground was shooting toward her at an astonishing rate. The kite kept spinning. The cliff face rushed past. It all blurred into one terrifying kaleidoscope of horror.

"Pull the cord! Pull the cord!" she heard again. Now it wasn't just the prince. Everyone was yelling.

Samantha reached up and yanked the cord. At first it didn't appear as though she'd been released, for she was still hurtling toward the rocks. Then she flapped her wings and on impulse performed a blowfly back flip, a full reverse-loop with a half-twist. Moments later, the kite crashed with a sickening *crunch*! into the base of the cliff.

Samantha landed on the ground faster than she anticipated and collapsed into a heap. The prince was the first to her side, cradling her to his chest, asking if she was all right, demanding that she respond.

Through the slits of half-opened eyes, Samantha saw everyone crowding over her, all talking at the same time, asking each other whether she was dead or alive. Even the king was there. He was the only one not talking, his expression grave. Then the prince said something else, just as she felt herself beginning to faint.

His distraught face was the last thing she remembered before blackness descended.

Samantha awoke with a start in her chamber later that evening. At first disorientated and feeling a little worse for wear, the memory of what had happened flashed across her mind. She rubbed a throbbing wing as she slipped out of bed.

"You've been through worse," she muttered, heading for the door. "There's no time to feel sorry for yourself."

When she arrived at the factory cave, Mad Jack and the prince were huddled over the wreckage of the flying machine, oblivious to her. She went over to examine the broken pieces. The cross poles had snapped and the wing-sheet was torn in numerous places, a complete catastrophe.

"Samantha, what are you doing here?" said the prince. Mad Jack jumped as if he'd seen a monster from the Crazy Lands. "You should be..."

Samantha shot a look that cut him short. At that moment, from across the lake, a blackbird chirped its night song: "To bed! To bed! To bed! The day is old. The night is cold. To bed! To bed! To bed!"

She recalled its graceful flight earlier that day, and it suddenly struck her that she knew what had gone wrong with the test flight. "I think I can fix the problem," she said.

The prince shook his head. "I hope you're not contemplating what I think you are."

"Of course I am. We're going to rebuild the kite. Only this time we're going to improve it. Make some modifications. It needs to be more aerodynamically stable, to counter any sudden wind shifts. We need to attach a long tail to stabilize the kite in flight, just like the tail of a blackbird. I'll get Lizzie started on it tonight."

She picked up some blocks of honeywood that Mad Jack had collected and selected three pieces suitable for what she needed. "The most frightening aspect of the spin was the helplessness," she said, handing the wood to the prince. "There was nothing to steer with. I want you to make a triangular frame in the shape of a capital A and lash it to the crossbeams. If I encounter another sudden downshift like this morning, I can steer the kite out of the spin."

The prince considered her ideas for a moment. "Very well, Samantha, I'll do this for you," he said, "and I'll even mend the broken poles, too. But it's not you who'll fly this kite; it will be me. I'll not allow you to risk your life again."

"But you can't even fly. If the kite crashes again, you can't buzz away like I did. You'll be killed."

He crossed his antennae in a manner that said he'd made his decision. Samantha relented, but quickly thought of an idea that might appeal to him – tandem harnesses. That way, she said, she could instruct him how to pilot the kite.

The prince reluctantly agreed, and the whole of the following day was spent fixing the kite and attending design modifications. Mad Jack helped Lizzie to make the tail, tying ribbons of denim and silk to a long piece of cotton string. Samantha patched the rips in the wing-sheet and modified Lizzie's overalls for the second harness. The prince lashed the broken poles together and constructed the steering mechanism, what Samantha called the A-frame. The conversation, however, was solemn; nobody dared mention the crash for fear of invoking bad luck.

The next day, after a short, fitful sleep, Samantha made the final touches to the flying machine. The tail was connected, as was the A-frame and the second harness. Everything was now ready.

With help from Mad Jack and Lizzie, Samantha and the prince slipped into their harnesses and shuffled to the mouth of the cave. Once again, Samantha peered over the precipice. The prince had managed to persuade the king, against his wishes, to attend the second test flight. He and the queen, along with several guards and a few of the prince's hunting party, were gathered around the barrel-pulley, staring up with worried frowns. There were no smiles or laughing or waving this time.

"Are you ready, prince?" Samantha asked. He looked as troubled and nervous as those below. "We don't have to do it if you don't want to."

"Samantha, if I don't do this then the bees in my hive will never have the chance to fly again." He leaned over and rubbed antennae. "If I'm going to die, at least I die flying."

Without further ado, Samantha stepped off the edge with the prince. The kite dipped toward the rocks and watching crowd for a frightening second, but then, as before, was swept high above the cliff on a gust of wind. Samantha felt a jolt through her harness as the rope wound off the barrel-pulley to the last loop, anchoring the kite. The prince was stunned into silence.

Suddenly, as had happened previously, the wind changed direction, sending them toward the rocks. The rope slackened. The kite dived and began spiraling down, narrowly missing the face of the cliff. Samantha heard faint gasps of horror from below, but she'd been prepared for this. Calmly, she steered the A-frame and brought the kite out of its spin. Almost immediately, they were lifted back atop the cliff on the next upward draft.

"You did it!" the prince said, amid the cheers from the ground. "We're flying! We're really flying!" He waved to the queen and king and they waved back.

For the next twenty minutes Samantha taught the prince how to pilot the kite. Soon he was as proficient as she, steering the kite this way and that, floating on the wind like someone who'd done it his whole life. Down below, Mad Jack had already joined the others at the barrel-pulley, so Samantha gave him the signal to winch them to the ground.

"Reet Bee-teet!" she said, as they descended. "I almost can't believe it."

"Aye, you better believe it," the prince said. "You don't know what this means to Beebylon. My father will soon be flying and we owe it all to you." The prince then rubbed her antennae and whispered the words that made her heart flip and somersault, like the kite had done when it crashed. "I love you."

Samantha now had no more doubts as to what Bee Dream she had found at the lake.

THERE WAS MUCH cheer in the hive of Beebylon from that day on. Word spread like ants to honey that the prince, with the help of a mysterious stranger, had built a magnificent flying machine. "The king will fly once again!" the bees said in the taverns and the markets and the hive-cells. "The king will fly!" There was an atmosphere of hope that even the old timers said was beyond anything they'd ever experienced.

Queen Beelinda and King Bernard organized a magnificent feast in the throne room for their son and his newfound friends. There were many royal cousins and dignitaries that Samantha hadn't met before. Sitting at the royal table, the king seemed merry enough. He had visibly changed, having shed the gloom that he had worn like a crown of thorns for many, many years.

"It's as if he's a young prince again," she said to Prince Robbee.

"Aye, indeed," he said. "He sits more erect and holds his head more proudly than before. 'Tis all for the good."

Toward the end of the feast, the king made an announcement. The flight would take place in two day's time. A loud cheer rang around the room. "It will be a momentous occasion," he said, and went on to make a grand speech that was full of wisdom and gratitude. In summing up, he said, "For the one thing I've learned in all these years is this: when we give up on what we're born to bee, our Bee Dream gives up on us."

Another cheer rang around the room. Suddenly, while everyone else was cheering and clapping and saying what a wise old bee the king was, Samantha saw Lizzie go rigid and quiet. Then she got to her feet, rather excited about something, and said, "I understand!" No one else could hear her above the celebrations, even though she was almost shouting. "I understand! I understand!"

"Calm down, Lizzie, calm down!" Samantha said, grabbing her arm and trying to pull her back to her seat. "What is it? What do you understand?"

Lizzie resisted Samantha's efforts to make her sit. "It's so obvious!" she said, clasping her chest. "I know why caterpillars count their steps! I understand it all! I know what I have to do. I'll be back."

Before Samantha could reply, Lizzie was gone; and by the time she retired to her bed-cell, Lizzie was still nowhere to be seen. Even when the prince came to her the next morning at the factory cave and told her the bad news, she refused to believe it. His hunting party had searched all night for her. Nobody had seen her. She'd just disappeared.

Samantha could only surmise that Lizzie had returned to the anthill. It was, after all, the place where she had felt most secure. It saddened her to think that Lizzie had turned her back on her destiny, just when she was so close to fulfilling it. That was something Samantha wouldn't do. Tomorrow was the culmination of everything she'd worked for. She would prepare for it as best she could, whether or not Lizzie was there to share the occasion.

Nevertheless, she slept poorly that night.

THE FOLLOWING DAY, every single bee in Beebylon gathered at the base of the cliff to watch history in the making, an occasion that was likely to never be repeated. Nobody wanted to miss a single moment, most arriving before dawn to get the best position. Some sat in the pine trees closest to the shoreline, others on someone's shoulder, some even set up sun shades and made a picnic. A marching band paraded back and forth and played all the crowd favorites, like "Rule Beetania" and "Goddess save the Bees". Moreover, to everyone's delight, even the famous soprano, Madam Butterfly, made a rare appearance and sang an aria or two. There was much flag waving and general bonhomie.

After she had checked the kite for the seventh or eighth time, the prince told Samantha that everything in the factory was under control. The king was strapped into the harness. There were royal guards to help lift the kite. There was nothing more she could do. Samantha reluctantly decided to go down and check the pulley, which Mad Jack was currently taking care of. She rubbed antennae with the prince and wished him and the king the best of luck. Then, with one last look over her wings, she went to the base of the cliff and relieved Mad Jack of his duties.

"Let me just give the pulley another check," she said above the noise of the ever-increasing crowd. It was almost noon, but you wouldn't know it, less than ten minutes before the scheduled takeoff. "The last thing we want is for the kite to lose control with the king on board."

"Don't worry yourself so much," Mad Jack said, looking very dapper in a new pair of silk overalls. Several honeystone rings also adorned his claws, Samantha noticed, and he even wore a honeystone medallion around his neck. "Everything will be just fine. You trained the prince well. The king will be safe."

Queen Beelinda had already taken her throne on the platform of the royal box, flanked by several royal guards. A south-easterly breeze flapped the gold and black flags above her. Samantha glanced up at them, then at the sky. Grey clouds slipped across the heavens rather too quickly for her liking.

"There's a storm brewing," her instructor at aerobatic flying school used to say whenever the clouds

161

raced each other like that. "Fold in those wings and take shelter. There'll be no flying today."

"I don't like the look of the weather," she said to Mad Jack.

Mad Jack followed her gaze to the heavens. "It's just a minor change," he said, and nodded to the crowd. "D'you really want to postpone the flight?"

Before she could tell him that that wouldn't be such a bad idea, trumpets blared from below the royal box. The crowd suddenly hushed and craned their necks toward the factory cave. Strapped into their harnesses, Prince Robbee and the king were standing on the precipice, the kite lifted from their backs by two guards. A dark shadow fell upon the cliff as a large cloud covered the sun. Samantha glanced up again, hoping she was wrong about the oncoming front. The prince was right; there was nothing more she could do. Except pray.

"Everything happens for a reason," she told herself. She just had to keep believing that.

She saw Prince Robbee and the king shuffle to the precipice and ready themselves. One more step and they'd be over. An excited hum passed over the spectators, but Samantha could barely watch. Then just as the shadow lifted and sunlight lit the face of the cliff, they dropped. They fell toward the rocks for what seemed an eternity, the same rocks that had been the cause of all of Beebylon's misery. The crowd groaned and Samantha held her breath. Then the wind gusted and the kite was lifted up.

Samantha heard the crowd take a sharp intake of collective breath. The kite soared toward the clouds, dragging its tether behind. The barrel-pulley spun like a bobbin, and from the centre of the crowd someone yelled, "The king is flying! Hail to the king! The king is flying!"

The crowd then let out an extraordinary cheer. Everything they had ever dreamed of was coming true before their very eyes. They kept waving and hugging and cheering, "Hail to the king! The king is flying! Hail to the king!"

Up and up and up the kite went, climbing at an incredible rate. The barrel-pulley kept spinning as the rope unwound, suddenly terrifying Samantha. She knew she had to act swiftly to prevent a horrible disaster from happening. She tried to grab the rope, but it was unwinding too fast.

"Help me!" she shouted to Mad Jack. "We have to slow the rope!"

Like everyone else, Mad Jack was so engrossed with the kite he didn't hear her frantic shouts.

Then Samantha's worst fears became a reality. She saw it all in slow motion. The rope unwound to its final loop and jerked to a halt, straining the knot. For a brief moment it held, but the sheer thrust of the kite's ascent was too great. It tugged the knot loose and the rope slipped off the barrel-pulley, dragging along the ground like a slithering asp. Samantha squealed in horror. She snatched at the free end, but she'd reacted too slowly and the rope slipped out of reach.

Mad Jack turned and saw what had happened. Now also aware of the danger, he jumped on the rope, just as a gust of wind lifted the kite higher. He was lifted into the air, dangling like a spider on the end of its thread. Samantha jumped up and caught him by the legs, almost pulling off his overalls, but the added weight of her body was too much and he could no longer keep his grip. He let go and fell on top of her, and they collapsed on the ground in a heap of wings and legs and arms. To her dismay, the kite soared higher toward the clouds.

At the royal box and around the base of the cliff, bees were still hugging and clapping, oblivious to the unfolding tragedy. "The king is flying! The king is flying!" they yelled.

Some of the nearby crowd, however, distracted by the commotion around the barrel-pulley, were now staring dumbfounded at the unfolding events. They gaped at the un-tethered rope, then up at the kite, which was now a rapidly diminishing blue speck against the grey backdrop, then at Samantha and Mad Jack, then back up at the kite again. They started pointing, telling their friends and neighbors what they'd just seen. A hum of disbelief replaced the cheers of joy, spreading through the crowd like ripples from a stone tossed into the lake. Within minutes everyone knew what had happened. They had come to watch the king fly again, to celebrate his glorious triumph. Instead, they were witnessing a catastrophe.

Then, Samantha saw, every face in the crowd began turning toward her.

SAMANTHA AND MAD JACK picked themselves off the ground. She didn't like the look of the crowd. There was fury in their eyes. Saying nothing, she grabbed Mad Jack's arm and took a step backward, but the crowd, looking more and more like a lynch mob with every passing second, had already formed a circle, trapping them. She could hear an angry hum from all sides.

At that moment, overhead, Samantha heard her name being called. The voice sounded familiar. She looked up and saw the most elegant and graceful butterfly she could ever remember seeing, even more so than Madam Butterfly, the soprano. The butterfly's wings were like royal silk, ruby and gold and jade. They seemed to shimmer in the grey light of day with an aura of their own, and Samantha's jaw dropped at the sight of such exquisite loveliness. The crowd stopped and stared as well.

"Do you not recognize your own friend?" said the butterfly.

Forgetting momentarily about the angry faces, Samantha's jaw dropped even further. "Lizzie?" she said. "You... you look beautiful!"

Lizzie kept hovering overhead like a goddess. "When I heard the king's speech, I finally realized what I was meant to do," she said. "I simply had to be a caterpillar. And caterpillars, you once told me, make the most beautiful chrysalises in the world."

While Samantha was still staring in amazement, a drone in the crowd made a grab for her. "Get her!" he yelled. "She's killed the king!"

Samantha yelped and, acting purely on impulse, buzzed into the air, just escaping his snatching claws. Before she knew what she'd done, she was hovering next to Lizzie. The crowd gasped.

"She's flying!" the drone shouted, pointing up. "Somebody arrest her!"

Nobody listened, not even the guards, although two of them grabbed Mad Jack and pinned him to the ground. He squirmed and wiggled and shouted that he was innocent, to no avail.

Samantha stared beneath her feet at the mob. Infuriated faces stared back up, seemingly half the gathering, thousands and thousands of them. They began humming louder, like a swarm of infuriated hornets. The ringleader, now shouting accusations and rather unpleasant things that were simply not true, threw a small rock at her, but it missed by quite a distance.

"Don't you have something to do?" Lizzie asked.

Samantha glanced beyond the waterfall where she'd last seen the kite. There were just grey clouds speeding across the sky. "What about you?" she asked, as another rock flew past her wings. "Aren't you breaking the law, too?"

"Only bees are forbidden to fly," Lizzie said. "Go now. Do what you were born to do. Be a bee."

Two or three rocks flew past Samantha's face. Without waiting for one to find is mark, she buzzed off, using the wind to push her on. Soon she was well above the cliff, higher than she had taken the kite on the test flights. The waterfall rushed over the precipice to the lake and the crowd. The bees were now as tiny as grains of sand on the shoreline. She surged forward, heading west toward the mountains where the river stemmed, where she feared the kite was being blown. That's if they didn't crash, a big IF; and even if they did manage to land safely, the king was too old to walk such long distances back to the hive and the prince would never leave him behind. Beebylon would never again see its king and prince.

Not if I've got anything to do with it first, she thought, now flying faster and higher than she had ever thought possible.

She scanned for the kite, using the air currents to determine the direction she should take. She assumed the kite was completely at the mercy of the wind, an assumption that quickly proved correct. There, against the grey clouds, she saw the blue diamond, out of control. The long tether dangled beneath it like the forelegs of a wasp, swaying back and forth as the kite's erratic flight jerked this way

166

and that. One second it was gliding high. The next, it was sent plummeting. Only the brave efforts of Prince Robbee were preventing it from spiraling out of control.

Spurred on, she made a beeline for it, buzzing as fast as she could. Just at that moment, a gust of wind pushed her forward, giving her an idea. The gap quickly closed. She grabbed the free end of the tether and buzzed up to the twin harnesses. In the chaos of trying to control the kite, neither the king nor the prince had seen her. Their eyes widened in surprise.

"Samantha, go!" the prince shouted above the wind. "It's too dangerous!"

Samantha ignored his protests and tied the end of the tether around her waist. She heard the prince shouting not to be so foolish, that if they crashed, she would be dragged down with them. Once again, Samantha ignored him. She was feeling suddenly courageous. If it were her fate to die with the prince, then so be it. She didn't want to imagine her life without him, anyway.

"I know how to get you down," she shouted back. "You mustn't fight the wind. If you do, you'll lose. You have to flow with it. I'll help you turn the kite around."

The prince understood at once, and nodded.

She buzzed away until the rope was taut. With all her might she pulled the kite in a wide arc toward the lake and Beebylon. Then began the slow tug back. She learned how to anticipate the airwaves, using the wind instead of fighting against it, waiting for a gust to push them the way she wanted to go, not resisting when it changed bearing. It was hard labor, two flaps forward, one flap back, but they were going in the right direction.

The prince also began to master the wind and the craft, learning to work in harmony with her. When the tether slackened, Samantha felt him glide the kite to tauten it again; and when the reverse happened, when she felt the tether tightening and her forward momentum beginning to slow to a halt, the prince somehow maneuvered the kite to ease the strain. This way, tightening and slackening, to-ing and fro-ing, they eventually zigzagged back to the waterfall.

"Well done, Samantha!" the prince yelled in sight of the lake. "We're almost there!"

The river rushed over the top of the cliff. Though her view of the crowd was obscured, Samantha felt a surge of relief. When they saw that she had saved the king and prince, she was sure to be forgiven. As she began her descent, Samantha felt a wave of air push her forward and the tether slackening around her waist. She looked over and saw the prince. He had brought the kite down close beside her. Like him, the king was smiling.

"Look, Samantha!" the prince shouted, and pointed to the flapping wing-sheet. "Kite gliding!"

Samantha laughed, and the prince told her to untie the rope from her waist. He was going to try and land the kite by himself. It was the safest thing to do.

Samantha complied, and once freed from the tether buzzed to base of the cliff. The waiting crowd parted as she landed. She'd done it. She had saved the king and he could fly again, like he had as a young prince. The law forbidding flight would be revoked, and Beebylon's future was assured. She hadn't felt this good since she was a wee grub tasting honey for the first time.

"Grab her!" the ringleader shouted. "Don't let her get away this time!"

The crowd surged in from all sides. Before she could buzz away again, Samantha felt several large claws grabbing her arms and legs and wings. She looked up to the sky, wondering what on earth had happened to the king and the prince. The kite was nowhere to be seen. "But... but..." she said.

"Be quiet!" a royal guard said, looming over her. It suddenly seemed darker. "You can answer to the queen."

He then nodded to her captors. Four guards marched Samantha through the pressing bodies to the royal box. The crowd booed and hissed and threw sand at her when she passed. Some bees snatched at her wings and antennae, calling her names. Such was her daze, she barely noticed.

"Hang the murderer!" an old drone yelled. "Hang her high!"

The guards marched her up the royal steps to the throne. Mad Jack was there, she saw, two burly guards at his side. His whole body was trembling. She tried to smile reassuringly, but it had as little power and warmth as the cloud-covered sun. The captain told her to kneel before Her Majesty, and prodded her between her wings with his stinger.

Samantha got on her knees, head bowed in shame. The queen said nothing for a while, as if torn between executing her on the spot or waiting until a trial was convened. The crowd booed and jeered from beneath the royal box. Sand rained down upon her and an empty lavender sac flopped onto the platform like a deflated cocoon. The captain turned to the crowd and ordered them to quit it. The throwing ceased, but there was still an angry hum.

Samantha looked up at Queen Beelinda, who was still motionless. The black and gold flags had fallen limp behind her. Then the queen drew a deep breath and gestured for the crowd to be silent.

"It seems we have misjudged you, Samantha Honeycomb," she said. "We trusted you with the life of our king and prince. You have betrayed that trust, and there is only one punishment for such treason."

"Hang her!" screamed the ringleader, worming to the front of the crowd. "Hang her high!"

The crowd roared with approval and a black wave of depression washed over Samantha's soul. The prince must have crashed the kite. It was the only reason why he wasn't here to stop this.

The queen held up her claw for silence. "And so Samantha, I do hereby order the royal guards to take you from this place..."

A frightful holler from above suddenly cut her short. "Stop! Stop at once!"

Every bee in the crowd looked up to see who had interrupted the queen. To Samantha's surprise, the king was dangling beneath Lizzie the butterfly, held tightly in her arms. Next to them was the prince. He was buzzing! A touch awkwardly, Samantha admitted, but flying nonetheless.

"Stop!" the king shouted. "Stop everything!"

The bees were stunned into silence. Even the rush of the waterfall seemed quieter than normal.

Then, after a second or two, someone deep in the crowd spoke up. "The king's alive!" Her voice was soft and disbelieving, but it carried easily to Samantha through the silence. "The king's alive!" she said again, this time louder. Then she shouted. "The king's alive!"

As if stung into action, a deafening cheer roared from the crowd. The bees jumped for joy, hugging and patting each other on the back, even strangers. "Hail to the king! The king's alive!" they shouted.

The crowd then parted as Lizzie gently landed near the royal box and released the king. The prince soon followed, landing a little clumsily. Some eager subjects helped him to his feet while the king hurried as fast as he could up the steps to the queen. The prince followed, and went straight to Samantha, who was still in a state of shock.

"It was too dangerous to land down here with the crowd and the rocks," the prince said, taking her claws and lifting her to her feet. "So I landed next to the river above the cliff. Lizzie came and told us what was happening."

Samantha looked at Lizzie, who fluttered her beautiful wings and nodded. Mad Jack just stared, for the moment too dazed for words.

"It's wonderful," the prince continued. "The king can fly. The law is immediately revoked. Beebylon is saved."

The king then went to the edge of the royal box and addressed the crowd. "This is a glorious day in the history of Beebylon," he said. "I pronounce this day a holiday, henceforth known as Flying Day!"

The announcement was greeted with a loud, joyous cheer. Prince Robbee stepped forward and whispered something in the king and queen's ear. They both nodded. Samantha watched in surprise as the prince bent down in front of her and took her claw. The crowd quickly hushed. Mad Jack kept staring as he had.

"Miss Samantha Honeycomb," the prince said, the crowd hanging on his every word, "I would be greatly honored if you should accept my claw in marriage."

Samantha gasped. Suddenly, as she stared at him, it all became clear to her: *Everything that had happened in her life had happened for a reason.*

She had said this often enough, but this time she *felt* it, a deep certainty that surged through her body like the blood in her veins. Everything – the crimson rose, Hive Prison, her exile, Gerald The Great, the ants, the flying machine – absolutely everything, had been in preparation for this moment, her Bee Dream. Like the connection between honeywood and honeyroot, she now understood that mysterious link between herself and the Great Mother.

To bee or not to bee, she heard the old actress in her head. That had always been the question. Now she had found the answer.

She glanced at the waterfall and the crowd at the base of the cliff. Every bee was humming with expectation. Lizzie continued to flutter divinely overhead. Mad jack was still speechless. Just then, the sun burst through a patch of cloud, catching her eye. It cast a bright halo around the prince, and for the moment he looked as beautiful as a golden sunflower.

"Aye, my prince, my hero," she said, gazing at him. "It is my honor to accept."

The crowd went wild, roaring with joy. Bees hugged and slapped each other between the wings. Some even buzzed into the air, falling back to the ground in surprise at what they'd done. The prince then stood and went to address the crowd, still holding Samantha's claw. The crowd roared as they approached. He gestured for silence and they hushed, though a low hum of expectation still rippled to Samantha's ears.

"I hereby present to you the future princess of Beebylon," he said, showing off his bride-to-bee. "Miss Samantha B. Honeycomb."

The crowd roared as one, "Hail to the princess! Hail Samantha!"

The prince then flapped his wings and buzzed into the air, taking Samantha with him. She heard Mad Jack's voice above the cheering: "Reet Bee-teet, Samantha! You never stopped believing!"

And while the crowd danced and waved and yelled with glee, she and the prince flew toward the waterfall and the cliff, toward Beebylon and her Bee Dream.

EPILOGUE

THE MARRIAGE OF Princess Samantha and Prince Robbee was to be a celebration like no other, a truly joyous occasion. Samantha's parents were the first to be invited. Then Gerald The Great (his was sent on the wind, to wherever he was). Invitations were also sent to every other royal house in the four known queendoms, including Queen Beetrix Bee IV, who, Samantha discovered later, had asked her advisors upon delivery of the Royal Scroll just who in Hive-Heaven this upstart princess thought she was?

"I've not heard of her," she had said to the High Priestess. "Surely it belittles me to even consider attending this wedding."

The High Priestess thought otherwise. "It would do you no harm to visit the new princess," she said, "for one day she shall be queen and it is said that she has discovered the secret to Infinite Richness. Would it not be wise to make friends instead of enemies?"

So Queen Beetrix had traveled with her court and the High Priestess to the colony in the Crazy Lands to fulfill her duty, where Samantha received her guests in the throne room. It was obvious that Queen Beetrix at first had no idea who she was. But when their eyes met, Samantha could tell that Queen Beetrix suddenly remembered the young bee she'd imprisoned, then expelled from the hive.

Samantha held up her claws and clapped twice. At once a dozen servants rolled in six large barrels, standing them in front of the throne. "I have fulfilled your quest," she said to the queen, "and I present you with these barrels. Each is filled with honeystone gems. You are no longer subservient to the greed of the High Priestess."

The queen bowed her head in gratitude, and Samantha saw her smile ever so slightly. Behind the queen, the High Priestess gasped and clenched her claws in anger.

"Do you now see the Wonder of Existence," said Samantha, "that there is a Higher Reason than our own? That the Great Mother is always helping us to become the best that we can bee?"

And as she left the throne room to join her new husband at the banquet, Samantha made a quick prayer to the Great Mother. "Oh Great and Merciful One," she whispered. "Help me to keep marveling at thee."

AUTHOR'S NOTE

One evening toward the end of 2001, while the world was still recovering from the shock of mid-September, I put down the book I had finished reading and said to myself, "Gee, I could write that."

I was living in London at the time. Had given up my day job as a pediatrician to pursue my dream and write fulltime, and consequently had slipped almost overnight from a life of champagne and prawns to baked beans on toast and water (without ice, too, I might add). A simple story like Jonathan Livingston Seagull had a certain allure, you could say, to a struggling writer. It was simple. It was short. But more importantly, it had *sold*.

"You need a title," I muttered to myself (I don't start a book until I have a title, even if it isn't the one I go with at the end – quirky, maybe, but to me it's like having a child and then waiting until she's fifteen before you give her a name). I glanced back at the cover of the book next to me. The response was immediate: *Samantha Honeycomb Bee*.

Great. Not only did I have the title, I also had the main character. Simple.

Only it wasn't. That's all I had. I had no plot, and I had no other characters. My mind was blank, and there it stayed, stuck on the first page (page zero, actually, when you think about it), until, at least, a couple of months later when I was coerced (bribed, actually, with the promise of drinks and dinner at the local Indian) by my wife's cousin into attending an evening service at the only Dutch Reformed Church within nine hours flight. Of course, I went. What unpublished writer wouldn't sell his soul for a curry and a beer? Anyway, I tried to console myself,

I won't have to listen to a word. It'll be in Afrikaans. It's all double Dutch to me.

The minister that evening, alas, decided to give the sermon in English. God knows why. I rolled my eyes and shoved the book I had brought along for company back in the backpack, resigned to an hour of boredom. My wife's cousin was smiling. *Just you wait till we get out of here*, I thought, *I'm going to order starters as well as main. And dessert*.

Anyway, within seconds the minister began talking of people he knew who were struggling with their day-to-day lives. He had a friend who was so busy she felt all she was doing was running around and around in circles. My tired eyes blinked open. I suddenly had my second character, Busy Lizzie.

That's good, I mused. *That's actually very good*.

The minister then spoke of a friend who had no idea of what he wanted to do in life, that he was just drifting from day to day, not doing much, just a bit of this, a bit of that. My eyes grew wider. My third character (Derek was later deleted, but at the time I didn't know that). "A dragonfly. That's brilliant."

When the minister finally ended his sermon, I suddenly found myself cradling Samantha's extended family like a father who didn't know his wife was giving birth to sextuplets. Needless to say, the beer and curry tasted supremely good that night.

My only problem now, was the plot. I'm not one of those writers (as you probably gathered) who meticulously sculpts his work. I'm not a planner, by nature, more of a go-with-the-flow kind of guy. Outlines scare me. So do recipes and DIY manuals. They seem to be written with only the end result in mind, not the process itself, the "getting there", the journey, where most of the joy is to be found.

Still, that said, I guess it's a bit of a balance. A writer, whether he's a scrupulous outliner or laid-back journeyman, still needs to know where he's going. *If you don't know to which flower you wish to fly, then no wind is helpful*, Gerald The Great said.

Along comes Providence (as She does, when you least expect Her). Providence provides. That's Her nature. Though *Tales of the Dervishes*, by Idries Shah, was not what I'd been expecting as the answer to my dilemma. I really should have known better. *Everything happens for a reason*, Samantha would've said. I now believe it with my whole heart.

Like an orphan, the book was waiting for me. In fact, it had *chosen* me. The Soho market on Rupert Street has a second-hand book stall every Sunday, which is an absolute bonus for a writer living on Rupert Street. I'd often seen the book on the stand, and like many ignorant folk had ignored it out of intellectual snobbery. "You can 'av that for 'alf price, mate," the dealer said, picking it up. "A pound fifty."

A goddamn bargain. I kind of knew it at the time, and I certainly know it now; the book of traditional Sufi parables is one of my most precious (few?) possessions. Back then, the parables of *Fatima the Spinner and the Tent* and *The Wayward Princess* caught my immediate attention. Fatima the spinner, marooned and enslaved on the way to her destiny with the Emperor, and the wayward princess, exiled by her father, the king, for refusing to admit his supreme authority over her life, were the ultimate inspiration for Samantha's incredible journey.

And it has been an incredible journey. I just hope you've had as much joy from reading the story as I did from writing it.

Scott Zarcinas
January 2006

Coming Titles

THE GOLDEN CHALICE
Scott Zarcinas

Fleeing the dreaded plague that has struck his village, the orphaned Giacomo heads to the mountains and its mysterious Golden City in search of the Elixir of Life, the only thing that can save the village and the woman he loves. His quest brings him face to face with the Six Thieves, cunning enemies who will stop at nothing to see him fail, and even with the Angel of Death herself. In the tradition of The Pilgrim Chronicles set by *Samantha Honeycomb*, *The Golden Chalice* is a compelling adventure story of self-discovery.

DEVILLE'S CONTRACT
Scott Zarcinas

Louis Hugo DeVille, CEO of the giant pharmaceutical company, Global Resolutions Network, suffers a heart attack in his office, only to wake up in the underground tunnels of LeMont International Enterprises. Louis has been headhunted by The Boss of the mega-corporation to help restructure its flagging corporate image, with the promise of limitless power and money. There's only one catch. He must sign an unbreakable contract, one that will bind his services to The Boss for an awfully long time. For eternity.